MW00426112

# DOWN THE PRIMROSE PATH

Kjerstin Lie

*To my Soup Snake.*
*Thank you for your endless hours.*
*Your endless support (tech, design and otherwise).*
*Your endless encouragement and laughter.*
*You helped me, help myself.*

# PART ONE

*Tristan*

# CHAPTER 1

Tristan leaned heavily on the palm of her right arm, staring distractedly out of the finger print infested window pane. Rain streaked along the outside and trickled down in sloppy spiderwebbed lines. The wind bullied, shoved and shook, the trees in the early autumn day. Leaves jostled and tossed about, creating little piles at the trunks of the neighboring trees. They fluttered savagely to the ground and landed limply on the steadily dampening moss-covered ground. A mesmerizing rough and tumble of mother nature blowing lightly on the foliage.

Tristan moved her round grey eyes slowly to the equally circular clock above the classroom door, the heads of her fellow students dotting the lower edge of her vision and obscuring her direct line of sight to the door. Tucking a loose piece of damp wavy, blonde hair behind her ear, she crossed her eyes in tired agony.

The clock reads 7:34am, meaning Mr. Ashburn would

come strolling in through the heavy oak and pen marked door in just under 60 seconds. The second hands ticked slowly in anticipation of his arrival.

Mr. Ashburn always insisted on an analog clock in his room. You couldn't find anything but digital on the rest of the Hillvale High School campus. On the first day of class Mr. Ashburn had tottered on the corner of Sammy Leroy's desk, and covered the digital clock with a bold-faced analog. He proclaimed it was "great for the memory and aided learning".

At this, everyone had either sighed out loud or rolled their eyes with such gusto that they practically sighed on their own.

Tristan found the gesture charming. And the rest of the class found it beneficial on Friday's when they could literally count the seconds until their morning drama class was over.

Tristan quickly shook her now half-asleep arm out after putting the entire weight of her bobbing head there for a few moments while she reflected on her morning. The rain had been nice and refreshing on her bike ride in.

She loved that. The little pellets of rain smacking against her mug, her long hair fluttering behind her peppered by the clouds dribbling. As a kid, she liked riding through puddles and coming home drenched. Her mother would quickly but half-heartedly laugh and point to the bathroom, where Tristan would soak in the heat of a long shower, afterwards.

The rainy-day regimen was nostalgic for her because her and her brothers would always cuddle up with hot cocoa on the couch after those drenched days. They'd watch movies for the rest of the water-logged afternoon and relax. They didn't do it much anymore. Mainly because one of her brothers had moved out last fall for college and her younger brother was in his emo phase. He currently specialized in resenting his family and pretending they didn't exist. Tristan didn't take it personally, obviously, but she did miss his company when these cozy days rolled by.

The school year had just started a few weeks previously and currently the entire student body was buzzing with anticipation because homecoming was the following weekend. But Tristan had other reasons to be excited.

Reason being; the first semester of the year was spent in Mr. Ashburn's class first period drama class.

Now, the subject wasn't exactly Tristan's topic of choice, but she'd gladly read the SparkNotes and Wikipedia pages on the plays they analyzed. And happily volunteer for every in-class reading of dialogue.

Mr. Ashburn had become something of a hot commodity around school since his arrival the previous year. Many girls thought he was charming, handsome and dapper. While the guys simply didn't give him a second thought. They only saw him as a dorky, young and theater obsessed new teacher.

They weren't wrong, he was rather young. This was only his second year of teaching, so that made him, what? 26? At most. And maybe that's why Tristan had found an intense interest. Mr. Ashburn handled the attention from the young women students well, but he could often be found blushing and stuttering awkwardly during unwarranted attention, while eyelashes were batted in his direction. Harrison Ford in Indiana Jones style, just without "love you" actually smeared across their lids.

He was the type of teacher that wore blazers or vests over his button ups. Squared off, thick tortoiseshell glasses donned his thin face and slim fit slacks hung off his frame. The cropped hair complimented his delicate features and he could always be found with a cup of coffee in hand.

His passion for the arts was quite evident and he was humorous. And while he was a young teacher, the students seemed to be able to sense his passion and respected him for it. Well, usually. The typical description of him was varied, some students called him pompous and a try-hard hipster, but the female crowd usually called him handsome and passionate.

There was a click at the door, bringing Tristan back to reality. And Mr. Ashburn's small but eager face could be seen in the narrow rectangular square of the safety glass from the outside of the classroom. Pushing his glasses up and leaning in close to the door, arms full of books, binders and a coffee mug that read, "I put the lit in literature". He rammed his shoulder into the door trying to inch it open.

A girl at the front of the room squeaked lightly, jumped up and hustled to the door to help Mr. Ashburn shuffle his way into the class without dropping one of his tottering items.

"Ah, thanks Mallory! I appreciate it," he exclaims slipping through the door and making his way to the large desk near the window.

"You'd think after all this time, I'd finally have that *door* thing down, wouldn't you?" Mr. Ashburn chuckled lightly, carefully setting everything down.

Clapping hands together and smiling widely at the class, he assessed their excitement levels. Most of the students just stared back at him without joy. A boy next to Tristan yawned and the girl in front of her fumbled in her backpack for a pen. It was Friday, after all.

"Well, everyone, how are we doing this fine, fine, *blustery* morning?" he said with obvious eagerness.

Tristan sat up a bit taller and plastered a goofy grin on, hoping to seem like a well-rounded and enthused student. Prepped and ready to begin today's lesson!

A few people murmur about it being wet outside and one kid in the back of the class simply let his head drop to the desk in defeated response.

Mr. Ashburn barely waits for a response, already turning to face the white board and writing the topics for the day on the board and launches in to the discussion. They had been asked to read through a play and were starting critiques on the piece.

But Tristan was completely gone. She let her brain take off. She floated and glistened as she stared at Mr. Ashburn with a lopsided grin.

*He has such white teeth. How do you even get teeth that white and straight? I bet he has the cutest baby photos, I mean, he's adorable now, why not then? Wait, do babies have teeth?*

Tristan kept on with these thoughts for the remainder of their 57-minute class. This was standard practice in the life of Tristan Pedersen.

She'd become obsessed with people for small portions

of time. So immersed that she'd daydream and think incessantly about whatever her newest craze was. When she was a kid it was the main character from a Disney Channel show. Fan mail was sent almost daily, filled with tear stained notes and drawings, until her mother became tired of spending so much on postage stamps.

Later it was an unhealthy endearment with a boyband. Tristan ran a fanfiction page online where she inserted herself into their lives as tour manager. In this phase she picked up Photoshop and learned how to add herself, almost imperceptibly, into candid shots with the fellows she had found online. This fandom ended when the band disbanded, leaving her disappointed, but opening her heart for new interests.

And then Tristan found Mr. Ashburn. Smitten is a mild understatement. In this case, she was full on googly-eyes, pink hearts, bouquets of flowers, hazy sight, "he has no flaws" obsessed with Mr. Ashburn. The desire and curiosity Tristan had in Mr. Ashburn was different from the past. This time, Mr. Ashburn was a real person. He was in her life. In the flesh. Touchable, alive and accessible.

So, even though she wasn't usually super involved in school activities, this year was the year she'd be dusting off the ol' singing pipes and going out for the first semester musical. The decision came about when she learned Mr. Ashburn would be directing the play and therefore staying afterschool almost daily with the students. It was her chance to really get closer. Learn more.

The first hour of the day passed slowly and steadily, as drama students spouted off answers to Mr. Ashburn's questions and pencils scraped at paper, taking notes.

Suddenly the bell rang. Loud, clear, shrieking and completely jump-worthy, especially with Tristan in such a sleepy, dreamy state.

She shook her head quickly a bit, tossed her hair behind her right shoulder and swept her backpack off the ground. Without closing her notebook, she pushed everything in to her bag, zipped it up and threw it haphazardly over her back. The toss came as a surprise to the person behind her.

"Ow!"

"Oh!" Tristan spun around alarmingly fast, feeling guilty instantly, "Sorry Simon! I wasn't paying attention, are you alright?"

"All good, Miss Scatterbrain!" he smirked and feigned a distraught and pained face. "Have a good rest of your day, I hope you get more chances to fawn over Mr. A".

Simon winked and slid effortlessly out of class, leaving Tristan alone.

She rolled her eyes with a small smile. She'd known Simon for years, a troubled kid but insanely funny. And quite charming, as well. He's the kind of guy it's hard to stay mad at.

She fixed her bag onto her back, breathing raggedly with nerves and made her way up to Mr. Ashburn's desk, where he had finally taken a seat, hands entwined in his lap.

"DON'T FORGET EVERYONE, AUDITIONS FOR THE MUSICIAL ARE RIGHT AFTER SCHOOL. YOU GET EXTRA CREDIT FOR PARTCIPATING IN ANY WAY!", he hollered. His voiced drowned by the shuffling of papers. The dull roar from the noisy hall got louder every split second as students pushed the door open and it started to close and pushed open again. Tristan beelined for him.

"Thanks for class Mr. A, that was great. You really know your stuff!" gasped Tristan, tripping over her untied high-tops. She looked up at him smiling admiringly.

"Uh, thanks Tristan. If I didn't know better, I'd say you had fallen asleep with your eyes open" he ventured. Arching an eyebrow, so it could be seen over the top of his thick glasses and smirked.

Her heart sank, "Oh, no, no. Just distracted a bit, but I was also.... taking... a lot of it in?"

She rolled her eyes at herself internally. *Idiot,* she

thought, *you were totally goo-gooing over him and didn't get anything out of this.*

"Oh, alright! Have a good one. I need a refill" he mentioned to his empty coffee mug, "Guess I'll see you this afternoon!"

And with that, he swiveled in his chair to face his computer screen and left Tristan standing awkwardly behind him. She hitched up her bag with a little bounce and sighed. She tossed her hair once more over her shoulder and braved the busy hallways to head to her next class, tripping over her laces the whole way there.

# CHAPTER 2

The rest of Tristan's morning flew by in a whirlwind of papers, discussions, group projects and assignments. Stumbling her way lazily to the next few classes, plopping in and out of plastic grey chairs with missing foot stops and squeaky seats.

In chemistry Simon sat next to her, as all lab partners do.

"Dude, chill! You're driving me nuts with that uneven chair" he said as she tipped the crooked chair backward and forward distractedly on the linoleum floors.

"Finally," whispered the girl in front of her, distain in her voice and a sharp eye roll.

Tristan simply raised her eyebrow and stuck her tongue out at the girl when she turned her back to face the front of the room, while Simon  stifled  laughter. Somehow Simon always seemed to be around to catch Tristan doing petty  and  embarrassing  things.  Then  again,  that  was inevitable. Growing up together had brought on more embarrassing memories than either of them would like to admit.

Simon had always been friends with her brothers and their mothers were in the same book club. So, they ended up together at friends' functions frequently. He was a nice presence to have around, Tristan noted, as they huddled together with two other Juniors to talk about the big group project that was required for the semester. She leaned in to the table to read their shared notebook.

The group finished doing some planning for the project before finally giving up on working in class on a Friday. They were tapped out and ready for lunch, anyway. The teachers who have class before lunch always got the least amount of attention out of the students.

"Did you hear about Scott? The band kid? What does he play? Drums, right?" Simon directed at his group, as he tipped back in his chair, while slightly smiling at the front of the class room, craning his neck as he saw someone walk by the window. He saw what appeared to be a person. And not just any person, but Lyss Rogers, drama queen extraordinaire. He started a little, his chair slid a bit too far and quickly propped himself back up. The terrifying moment of tilting your chair too far, everyone's greatest classroom fear.

"What about him? That he came out? Yeah, I heard. I'm a bit surprised, but like, also not" Sammy, one of their partners said pointedly, as she twirled her pencil in her curly hair. "I mean, either way, he's talented, and he's super nice. I'm glad he felt comfortable coming out. Ya know?"

"Agreed!" Tristan spouted, "I mean who cares, anyway. Now maybe he'll go to the dance with someone he's *actually* interested in! Can you imagine how nice must feel?"

Tristan, ever the optimist.

"Totally. I mean, I won't claim to know what that's like, but it's pretty damn cool. And it seems like everyone is accepting of it" Simon said while glancing at the clock. "Oh, shit. One minute 'til lunch. I'm packing up!"

He slammed his chair onto all fours again and scooped up his bag, there was no "packing up" necessary because none of them even took their notebooks out, except Sammy, who just tangled and untangled her pencil from her immense curls and stuffed their group work into her bag.

"Y'all have homecoming plans?" Simon said glancing up at Tristan.

"Nah, I don't think so. I mean, I'll go. But I don't have anything planned yet. 'Suppose I'll just go with Sierra and some friends. Milkshakes and movies after? The usual shit"

Tristan responded, "What about you?"

"Eh, no plans either. Maybe our crews can join forces?"

"I'm down. See ya later, man!" she smiled as the bell rang and the halls flooded with socially deprived, hungry teenagers.

Tristan swung her forest green Herschel backpack over her shoulder. She could hear all the loose, stuffed papers crumpling inside, as she tossed her bag on an empty circular table near the far side of the cafeteria, close to the windows. She wanted to claim their normal lunch table before someone else snagged it. It was a prime table, by the windows and foosball table.

*Shit,* she thought, *I really need to get organized. But for another time!* She knew that Sierra would be willing to help her get all organized this weekend if she asked her. That girl lived for binders and sticky notes and file folders with labels. Her bedroom was basically a Staples.

Tristan meandered over to the closest lunch line. She was more of a "snack" type of gal so always ordered random bit of carbs, cheese and sugar infused drinks.

"Afternoon missy! What are we doing today?" asked the friendly lunch server whose name was Theresa.

"Theresa, ma' girl. Hit me with the soft pretzel,

cheese, a bag of regular sun chips and a diet coke!"

"You got it, type your lunch number in while I get it. You know the drill" she smiled back and winked. She was a friendly middle-aged woman, big mouth, big eyes and beautifully black and wavy hair.

"Thanks!" sang Tristan over her shoulder as she skipped back to her reserved table.

"Hola, my friend" she said as she wiggled her shoulders and tossed her food on the table, spraying cheese into a few directions.

"Hey" Sierra said, looking up and giving her friend a knowing half-smile. "How's it going?"

"Gooooodddddddd, just had a wildly boring morning spent in all of my classes. Except for Ashburn's, of course." She tore open her bag of Sun Chips, with more force than necessary, and a few crumbly bits littered the table. Sierra wiped them away distractedly "and now here I am. How you do? What is all of this?" Tristan asked as she knit her brows together in confusion, gesturing to the mess in front of Sierra.

Sierra's book bag looked like it had exploded onto the rest of the table. Somehow Tristan had missed the explosion of items. There were markers, books, call lists, ribbons, posters, binders and a hundred more items scattered about the table. Tristan gaped and turned to her friend with an exasperated look.

"No. No, you can't do this at lunch. C'mon. This is crazy! You're going to go insane." Tristan said, as realization dawned.

Sierra was the ASB President of the school and rightly so. The girl could organize anything. She could convince anyone to help her and was so on top of things it made Tristan look like an infant trying to fly a broom. Clumsy and confused.

This was probably why Tristan and Sierra were such good friends. They had a lot of the same opinions, but they functioned completely different. Tristan flopped through her days, tossing her long blonde curtain of hair around and fumbling along with a "fuck it, it's easier to be happy" attitude. Whereas, Sierra was a planner. Her whole life revolved around excluding *spontaneity* from her vocabulary, but damn was she smart. She was a control freak, with quick wit, lots of ideas and the girl was stunning. Natural brunette curls, angular face and the tiniest waist line. Most girls were not only jealous of her success, but of her body, too. The girl applied drug store makeup like she was Laura Mercier herself. She worked little on her hair and she never seemed to gain any weight, despite the amounts of burgers Tristan saw her shove down her throat.

But, in Tristan's opinion, Sierra was a bit unhealthy with the whole thing. She stressed herself out to the point where she didn't sleep. She looked like a zombie half the time, but Tristan only thought so because she was so close with her. Sierra could be quick to anger when she was working on a project, and she often looked like she was sleeping with *her* eyes open.

"T, don't worry!" Sierra blinked innocently back at her. "I'm working on the homecoming dance. It needs to get done. I'm just reviewing my details. We have the big meeting tonight. The more prepared I am, the sooner the weekend can truly begin".

Tristan glared at her as she dunked her pretzel into her cheese and shoved it into her mouth.

"Or-kay. Bu' as soon a' this dan-ce i' ov'r" she swallowed her food, "we're spending the *wholllllleeeeee* next weekend watching movies, stuffing our faces with chocolate and stalking celebrities on Instagram"

"Deal" beamed Sierra, "Okay, so tell me more about Ashburn while I'm working on this. I want the details. How's that cutie-pie doing? Your eyes light up every time you or someone else mentions him... so I'm dying to hear about your torrid love affairs", she flourishes her hand full of flyers around to exude more drama than necessary.

"Alright, I'll distract you *and* myself. I'm happy to talk about the angel-faced drama teacher if I *have to*. He's so damn attractive. I mean really, I feel like when I look at him my vision is blurred with pink smoke. I'm like 90% sure my eyes start to bulge out when I'm in his class. Today he thought I was just zoning out, but I was actually just drooling over his perfection. Remember that scene from that short 'Red Hot Riding Hood', I am the wolf in that scenario.... but Mr. A isn't a hot woman in a red dress.... he's this swoon worthy, well-read drama professor" she laughed, completely aware of how creepy she was being.

Sierra cringed at her and laughed loudly.

Tristan told Sierra about class, about auditions that evening too.

"You're a great singer, Tristan. I hope you get the part, not just because you could hang out with Mr. A but also because it's a cool opportunity" Sierra said, nodding her head in support as she straightened a stack of papers.

"Thanks, I mean, I suppose you're right. Maybe it could be fun. Some of those girls in the drama department are funny, too. So at least it could be entertaining" Tristan mused.

Tristan had a musical family. Her brother was a guitar

player in some punk band at his college. They played every Friday and used their earnings to buy cheap beer for Saturday's. And Tristan's folks had made her take piano and voice lessons growing up. She was talented, but she didn't take it too seriously. She didn't take most things too seriously.

"Hey Sierra. Tristan, hey" said a voice from behind them.

Tristan looked over her shoulder and Sierra spun all the way around in her chair.

"Hey babe" Sierra said to Jay, with a smile and a quick wave to the girl next to him. Tristan was pretty sure the girl's name was Becca. Or maybe Amber? Everyone knew her because of her jealously inducing vibrant blue hair and her suspiciously non-romantic relationship with Jay.

Jay was the ASB Secretary and good friend of Tristan and Sierra's. He had lived across the street from Sierra since they were kids, so they often drove to school together and planned study groups for Sunday nights. Tristan didn't much like the study sessions but was happy to borrow Sierra's label maker for hours on end while they half-gossiped and half-studied.

"We still good for the meeting after school? Do you need anything from me before then?" he asked with a glimmer of a smile.

"Yup, meet in the ASB room, we can make all the posters and get the tickets all organized for the dance. I think I have almost everything else organized, so nothing necessary until this afternoon! It'll be fun. I think Mr. G is ordering pizza for us too, so even better" Sierra replied with a smile and a curt nod.

"Sweet! See ya after school then, don't work too hard, love" he smirked and gestured at their table.

"Also, I love those jeans on you, Sierra" said Jay's friend, Becca (or Amber?), "I wish I was thin enough to pull off high waisted jeans without my hips looking weird and lumpy".

Sierra half-smiled, "Thanks! I'm sure you'd look great too".

Becca shrugged, smiled and she and Jay took off.

*Beeeeeppppp*

"Alright, well shit. Lunch is over! Back to reality" Tristan picked her bag up off the floor.

"Yup, see you later? Movies this weekend?"

"Sure thing. And hey, did you eat?" Tristan rustled around in her bag and pulled out a semi-smashed granola bar. "Here, take this at least! I think it's chocolate, it'll hold you over until your pizza extravaganza after school".

"Awesome, thanks. You're a life saver. I'll catch up with you later!" Sierra started neatly stacking her piles of materials back up and put them delicately into her book bag.

Tristan waved, tossed her trash into the garage and bumbled her way back to class.

# CHAPTER 3

The rest of the school day was about normal as it could possibly be. More droning on from teachers, more jokes with classmates. Some writing assignments, but all in all, it was a Friday. Simple as that. Teachers and students alike are feeling particularly done and over the week. Teachers are looking forward to their evenings of wine and grading papers, while students couldn't wait to go to a party, relax at home and worry about their social lives instead of their grades in calculus for a few days.

The bell for the end of the day sounded, and all the students quickly packed up and made their way for the exits. Tristan, swept up her belongings, danced out of class and went in search of her friends.

She bumped into Sierra quickly since her last class of the day was in the same wing.

"Hey, hey" she exclaimed as she put her hand on Sierra's back.

"Hello! What have you got, fifteen minutes?" Sierra said with a tired grin.

"Yeah, just about. Wanted to dump these books in my locker and was gonna head to the arts wing after. You?"

"Same. Then heading to this ASB get together and then going to call it an early night, but I'm down to hang out this weekend!"

"I'm game. Let's chat this evening?" Tristan responded, as she stuck two thumbs up and wiggles them up and down, miming a rapid-fire text conversation. "I'll catch ya later. Have fun tonight!"

Tristan takes off down the hall, pops open her creaky locker. She snags her black hoodie and tosses her text books into the metal abyss. If there are books she'll need for homework this weekend, she'll just borrow them from Sierra. Hauling them all home at night on her bike seemed terrible, therefore not worth the work.

She bumps into some of the girls from the drama club and they chatter back and forth as they meander toward the arts wing. Smiles aplenty and excited gossip keeping silences from seeping through the conversation. They mostly talk about homecoming and how they would be wearing their hair, whose house they would do photos at and what color gloss would look best.

They flounce through the thick double doors that lead behind the stage to the theater. A pile of students gathered around, chatting, laughing and looking through scripts and sheet music together. Excitement and anxiousness filled the spaces between breaths and every student seemed to be feigning an air of confidence.

Tristan spotted a few of the more posh and popular girls from her grade. Including Lyss Rogers, the queen of the arts department. Homegirl was stunning, talented and was always chosen for the leads in the school performances. Tristan felt a twinge of nerves in the pit of her stomach, realizing that Lyss was her competition.

*I mean, I'd like to play the lead, I think. But if Lyss gets the part, it's not a big deal, I'll do set design or something,* Tristan thought. She wasn't someone who got nervous easily. But she hadn't spent much time singing in the last year since her brother left home, along with his guitar. So, she had no one to practice with.

After a few minutes, Mr. Ashburn came strolling through the door, whistling and smiling as he bounced on his feet.

"Hello everyone! Hello, hello," he hollered over the chatter, trying to gain their attention.

Tristan's heart skipped a beat, or maybe more than

skipped, it full on thumped against her chest and she coughed a bit. Mr. A had quite the effect on her.

"I'm so happy to see such a big turnout. It looks like we will be able to have a successful show with all of you and your help. But I'm sure the extra credit didn't help, did it" He beamed at everyone, as they shifted to see and listen to him. A few students guiltily chuckled at the last comment.

"Alright, I'm going to split groups up. If you are working on the set or lights and such, you should know where to go. I have Ms. Malone here to help with the art and design of the set and Mr. Crups to help with the lighting and all technical work. You know who you are if you're in those groups, so go ahead and go to them" he gestured lavishly to the far end of the stage where the other two teachers stood, coffees in hand and talking together in low voices. They both looked up and nodded affirming Mr. Ashburn's instructions to disperse but quickly settled back into their low conversation, waiting for the students to shift about.

"As for the rest of you, those who are trying out for the play, follow me, we're heading around to the stage and we'll do some audition work there".

The students split up and went to their spaces. And Tristan jumped at the chance to follow closely behind. She sat as close as she could to him, when he plopped into a seat in the audience with his clipboard and razor thin laptop propped on his knees. She tried to be subtle, but it was difficult when she was so excited to see him hard at work, in his element. She sighed and started in with her normal routine, which consisted mostly of staring at his darling, inspired face.

Mr. Ashburn wasted no time in starting the auditions. He paired people up for different parts, shifted them around, deciding whose voices blended well together. Finally, he called out for the leads. There were only a handful of people trying out.  Lyss was one going for the female lead and Tristan was the other.

Tristan could hear Lyss's group of friends whispering about her, but she tried her best to ignore their snarky comments and incessant giggles. She didn't want them to affect her or throw her off, since that was clearly their goal. This was a strategy she had picked up from growing up as the only female sibling. If you acknowledge their power and efforts, then they win automatically.

Tristan couldn't help but feel a slight flutter in her chest that she could only interpret as nerves. It wasn't the same flutter she got when her heart did jumping jacks as Mr. A looked right into her soul, it was different. It made her eyes dart back and forth and her palms sweat. She wrung her hands together and slapped a smile on, while Lyss made her way to the front of the group, ready to start her audition.

The girl had talent. Tristan watched in awe as she belted out the lyrics to the song, full of feelings and drama. She didn't look at the audience, she seemed to look just beyond. Lyss was zoned in, and sounded incredible, but she seemed to lack emotion and depth in her performance, Tristan noted. Her abilities to perform were undeniable. Her shiny hair was propped up perfectly on the top of her head, her leather jacket framing her curves smoothly. She was just so *cool*. Everyone envied Lyss, she had the best clothes, the best hair and boy was that girl driven.

Lyss's performance was followed with a small, polite applause from the students who listened. She smiled and confidently departed the stage, making sure to shoot a glare in Tristan's direction before sitting back down with her friends.

*I don't really stand a chance* Tristan thought to herself. *But man, it was worth trying that's for sure.*

She could feel herself getting competitive, another trait she developed in her youth full of bullying boys and endless hours of hot lava monster.

Plus, the idea of working closely with Mr. Ashburn made her palms start sweating all over again.

"Alright, Tristan! You ready?" Mr. Ashburn smiled,

then yawned as he leaned over his chair, clipboard in hand, and nodded his head in the direction of the stage.

Tristan wiped her moist hands on her jeans, pushed up the sleeves on her hoodie and pushed herself out of the stiff auditorium seats.

She grew up with the mentality that stress was a choice and that it's easier to just not take life so seriously. But this moment, in front of her peers, in front of Mr. Ashburn and his intrusive eyes and sharing her voice with others, that was scary. Tristan didn't have the performing background Lyss had, she wasn't in plays, she wasn't pursuing a career in performing arts, she just happened to have a knack for carrying out harmonies and making some pretty sounds alongside her brother.

"Whenever you're, uh, ready, Tristan, you can start" says Mr. Ashburn. And Tristan realizes she has just been standing in front of the group, completely zoned out and immersed in her thought.

"Oh! Yeah, yeah. Sorry" jumping to life, she mumbled as she shook her head and stretched her neck left to right.

Then, before she had a chance to think twice, she launched in to the song for the audition. Letting her eyes glaze over, as she stared into the crowd, she was certain she was creeping people out, but wasn't sure. She needed something to focus on. She kept her voice steady and tried to remember all the words properly. It's not like she practiced, she heard the song once or twice, and then listened to Lyss sing it as well. She wasn't even sure if she'd actually audition, she just thought of it as a neat opportunity. And then Sierra found out about it and was nothing shy of supportive. So, now here Tristan was, mid-song, starring at Mr. A while she sang a beautiful song for her school musical.

She could hardly remember starting the song, let alone finishing.

The group was quieter than it had been after Lyss sang. Less applause and no whispers of approval or otherwise. *Oh fuck*, she thought, *that bad, huh?*

"Tristan, thanks. That was, well, lovely" Mr. A sounded shocked. His eyebrows were raised, eyes wide.

*Shit, maybe I've lost my touch. It has been a while since I've sang...yikes.* She thought to herself.

Tristan gave a nervous smile and went to plop back in her seat near her buddies.

"Dude, what the hell was that?" one girl whispered to her. Tristan knit her brows together again, self-consciousness sneaking into her mind. She tugged at her sleeves and grimaced.

"Wha-what do you mean?" Tristan nervously stuttered

back at her, her confidence now completely drained. She had obviously embarrassed herself in front of the whole performance group. Not to mention Mr. Ashburn.

"No, I mean like, wow. That was incredible. I had no idea you could sing like that" she whispered back, her eyes as big as saucers with shock and surprise.

"Oh, thanks. I think. I hardly remember being up there" she responded, feeling her face burn.

"I mean you did stare at the audience a lot, which was a bit creepy, but it was a really emotional rendition".

"Thanks, I guess. That makes me feel better, I got pretty nervous".

"You? You're so dumb! You didn't look nervous at all".

Mr. Ashburn interrupted, "Alright, people! I will be chatting with the other faculty members and I'll be letting you know about the leads shortly! So, just hang out and we'll let you know about parts in a bit, that way you can start studying your lines and parts this weekend."

"Wow, already?" Tristan murmured.

She gathered with some other students from her class. A bunch of them mentioned that they really liked her audition. The sweat on her hands didn't subside as she got praise. It made her feel super awkward. She didn't really like the idea of being the center of attention.

The group continued to chat, make plans for the weekend and gossip about who was going with who to the homecoming dance the following weekend. Girls gestured at their hair while talking about their curls and updo's. There was talk of limos, dresses and where to get vodka because "I can't go to this dance *sober*".

Something like thirty minutes later Mr. Ashburn finally appeared with the other teachers, whose names completely evaded Tristan. The other arts teachers started to talk to their groups after getting them huddled together and Mr. Ashburn made a beeline for Lyss.

*Oh, great. I knew it. I made a total ass of myself. I guess I can always see Mr. A at rehearsals while I'm working backstage. That's something still. But damn, kind of a bummer.*

Tristan was only a little bothered. She didn't expect much in terms of getting somewhere with the musical, she had really convinced herself to audition for the sake of hanging out with Mr. Ashburn, but she was a little hurt. Ego wise. But what do you do?

She turned towards her friends and keeps chatting, distracting herself with idle chatter instead of focusing on the bummer supreme that just presented itself. Easier to move on than linger on the disappointment, she'd still have fun participating.

There is a bit of shuffling and the rising of voices coming from behind her. They can feel the heat and anger rising in the room as the tension builds, and Tristan spins around with everyone else to find a red-faced Lyss. Her brows dipping low, her teeth barred, and her fingers spread wide near her face as she starts to shout indignantly.

"YOU ARE KIDDING ME RIGHT? ACTUALLY, YOU'RE FUCKING JOKING," she spits in the direction of Mr. A, as he takes a step or two back, eyes wide and hands up as though he is surrendering.

"GOOD LUCK PUTTING ON A GOOD SHOW WITH YOUR COMMUNITY COLLEGE DEGREE AND SUB-PAR LEAD!" she gestures in the direction of Tristan, whose eyes dart side to side, confused.

*Lead?*

Lyss snatches up her coat and bag, shoves past her posse and storms out, letting the heavy oak door slam behind her, as the rest of the students stand in stunned silence. Their eyes on Mr. A's back, as he puts his left hand to his temple and takes a big sigh.

"Well, cats out of the bag" he gives a weary smile as he turns to face Tristan "Congrats Tristan, we are giving you the lead. You have a wonderful voice, you made the audience really *feel*. And with that ladies and gents, I'm just going to simply post the casting list on the back wall and you can all let yourself out. I am quite ready for the weekend, and I'm sure you'd all like to know what parts you were cast as".

And with that, he tacks the rest of the list to the back wall as student's swarm around and pat Tristan on the back as they pass her, muttering congrats and giving her grins as they head out.

Tristan is in shock.

*I got the lead? I get to be here every day? Work on this? Shit, that's incredible. But Lyss....*

"Sorry about all of the hub-bub Tristan," Mr. Ashburn says as he walks up behind her. "I was trying to ease the blow with Lyss, but apparently she didn't take it well. Hope you have a good weekend though, you and I will start working on blocking next week, so it may help to give your lines the once over this weekend!"

He pulls his coat over his shoulders, swings his bag around him and with a small wave, trots out of the room.

Leaving Tristan beaming.

# CHAPTER 4

The sun has nearly set by the time students begin to exit and make for home. It certainly feels like fall, as the brisk air sweeps past Tristan, blowing her long hair around her face and out behind her. She tugs at her hair, twists it up and tucks in behind her head, pulls up her hood and zips her sweatshirt as she tromps towards the bike racks. Still beaming with excitement after getting the lead role in the musical. She couldn't wait to text Sierra about the whole event.

Rustling around in her backpack for bike lights and tightening the straps on her bag so it crept up her back a bit higher to keep from bouncing while she rode.

Just as she was about to mount her sturdy, steel steed, she could make out Mr. Ashburn fumbling and jingling his set of car keys in the staff parking, which was adjacent to the bike racks. He had stacked a pile of books and his empty coffee mug on the top of his rusting Toyota Corolla.

*He's probably had that cruddy car since he started at college,* Tristan postulated. She watched him push up his thick square frames on his nose and toss his leather satchel into the passenger seat. He turned the car on, rubbed his hands together for a moment, while scrolling through his phone. He was lit up, and Tristan could make out every contour in his beautiful slim face. She sighed and smiled, recalling the situation back in the school.

He put the phone down and slid the car in to reverse. The car squeaked a bit as he turned the wheel, gracefully moved the car into drive and steered the hunk of metal out of the school parking lot.

As if by instinct, Tristan guided her bike smoothly behind Mr. A. Pedaling hard and fast, her breath twisting in the wind and drizzling rain. Her legs were strong from riding all over town for years. She muscled her way along, keeping a bit of distance but staying as close as possible.

Tristan pulls to a stop at the red light, seconds ago flickering into existence. Her eyes watch Mr. A's tail lights disappear around the corner. By the time the red glow had changed to green, his rundown car was nowhere to be seen.

*What am I doing?* Tristan shook her head, thinking to herself.

She pushed down hard with her right foot and crossed

the intersection. Looking for a trace of her prey. She had to make a choice and swinging onto Fowler Rd seem as good an option as any. Pedaling fast, she finally caught sight of the car, her decision had paid off.

He drove in the direction of some neighborhoods and apartment buildings that were popular and relatively close to the high school. He made a right turn into a quaint apartment complex, where he parked, snagged his bag and hustled inside.

Tristan, trailing behind, came to a stop at the corner of the entrance watching him fly in the front door. She was completely mesmerized, not thinking straight.

For a moment she shook herself out of her stupor, questioning her sanity, before shaking away the reservations and continuing towards the complex building.

Hopping off the bike and guiding it closer the entrance, she dropped it behind the thick stone sign that read "Whitewater Apartments" in big curly, fading letters. Two of the three outdoor lights that were supposed to be illuminating the sign were burned out.

The bike landed in the mushy beauty bark with a thud and tinkling sound as the pedal turned slightly from the movement. She tiptoed, or at least trying to, in the mud towards the building.

Mr. Ashburn had ducked into a unit on the corner bottom floor, closest to the entrance, lights from inside the apartment poured out on to the leafy, wet earth outside. What great luck that he lived on the lowest level. There were trees butting up closely to the building, which allowed Tristan some cover. She pushed through the bushes and branches before getting close to the window and its warm glow. She hadn't realized how cold it was until gazing through the steamy pane and taking in the cozy apartment.

She felt nervous. Her stomach churned, her heart thumped against the inside of her chest.

*What if he sees me? What would Mr. A do? Surely, he wouldn't want me in the play anymore...*

She crept as close to the window as she dared, standing on the rubber toe of her Converse and peering into what she found to be a small kitchen.

All white, with cheap laminate cabinets. Pictures and silly vacation magnets littered the fridge that sat across from the window. There was a pot on the stovetop, with thick steam billowing out and bubbles starting to crest the rim. Vegetables, all cut and diced in neat little piles on a massive cutting board, with a knife sitting atop a bright blue kitchen rag.

The warbling sound of voices and laughter. It sounded

like when the adults in Peanuts talk, just jumbled, muffled sounds instead of real words. Tristan stretched her neck a bit and put her fingers on the window sill ledge to pull herself up, trying to get a better look and saw movement, making her crouch down quickly to remain out of sight. Tristan's breath escalated, she was basically panting. Clasping her hands over her mouth and feeling the nerves rise up in her chest. She felt frozen, the voices became clearer, it appeared Mr. Ashburn was coming in to the kitchen, but with who?

*Maybe he has a roommate? He had never mentioned it in class. But why would he have mentioned it? It's probably an old college friend. How nice, living with your best friends.*

Tristan tried to listen and was able to make some bit of the conversation out through the thin single paned window. She continued to hold her breath.

"Today was rough. I'm so glad it's the end of the week, I don't think I could have handled another day without a break".

The light banging of pots and pans littered the background. Tristan built up the confidence to straighten back up and lean closer to the window, her lips tucked into her mouth and her brow furrowed. She couldn't wait to see how he looked at home! Her stomach tickled with mischievous excitement.

"Just a bunch of bitchy students, some talented kids at auditions, but man, this one girl just thinks she owns the place. It's so challenging. I fell legitimately attacked, but don't want to seem weak. It sometimes sucks when these kids know I'm only in my twenties because they think they can fight with me the same way they fight with their own friends. In high school, I had friends my current age who would buy me booze. Why would these students think any higher of me? UHG! Either way, how was your day? I don't want to whine! I'm sorry".

Tristan took that moment to peek through the window. Perplexed by his attitude about work. She found herself looking at a dainty, lovely young woman with a pixie cut and delicate features. The mystery woman swept her way toward Mr. Ashburn. Wrapping her arms around his shoulders.

"Babe! Don't stress, you can complain all you want. You know that. But to answer your question, my day was good. Had a decent time with these clients I've been working with. But I'm glad it's Friday night and I can hang with you now," she leaned in close to him as he set down a bottle of wine he'd been trying to uncork with frustration. Then held a long and sweet kiss. She pulled away smiling, turning around to grab her chopped veggies and glanced at the window.

She started.

*Oh, shit.*

"Hey! Oh my god! Hey! Babe, I think someone is outside the window!" she shrieked, pointing her painted nail at the window and looking terrified.

Tristan panicked. She started stepping backwards quickly as she heard Mr. A start stammering. She tripped over the root of a tree and put her hands back to brace the fall. Her left hand made contact with something sharp as it hit the squishy ground. She glanced down but didn't have time to process, jumping up she ran like crazy. Pulling her hood on tight and sprinting in the direction of the bike. Tristan snatched it up as she heard the front door slam open. Pedaling, pealing. Mr. A shouted into the night.

"Hey, who's there! I'm calling the cops!"

But he didn't see her. He couldn't have. She was in all black and forest green; her bike lights were off, and the sun was too deeply set to give her blurred figure away.

She panted and finally slowed as she turned a third corner to the left and it felt safe enough to take it easy on pedaling.

She hadn't turned her bike light back on for fear of being spotted. Coming to stop she leaned on the handlebars, catching her breath. Urging her pounding heart to slow down. After a few moments of calm, she turned toward the nearest street light. Making her way underneath, she finally flipped her hand over to assess the damage of her fall as she let her feet drag on the cement, slowing to a stop.

Walking and steering the bike while still sitting on it she saw her hand was covered in blood. A few small pieces of green glass were imbedded in the cut. She must have landed on a discarded beer bottle. Not something uncommon to find in the local woods and close to the high school. Grimacing she picked a few pieces out. Undoubtedly, she'd need to use tweezers when she got home to pick the rest out. Tristan swore at herself, pulled the sleeve of her hoodie over the wound to cover it as the cold wind picked up, making the cut sting.

Cringing she stopped herself all the way.

*What the hell was I thinking? I must be crazy...Mr. A isn't that great, he isn't worth getting in trouble for...or arrested over! But he has a girlfriend, he's never mentioned her. What did I expect though? I was being unsafe...crazy.*

Tristan blinked her big grey eyes a few times and looked around her. She was alone except for the wind, the rain and the leaves tousling along the ground all around her. The weather had officially switched to fall, she noted shivering and pushing her hood lower onto her head.

Tristan remembered she was supposed to make plans

for this weekend with Sierra, and at that moment, she saw movement ahead of her. She squinted into the dusky, water stained path ahead. There was an outline of a struggling shadow. Again, curiosity got the better of her and she hesitantly lifted herself back on her bike seat and slowly pushed off the ground to ease closer to the mysterious walker.

After all Tristan had endured on this strange Friday evening, why not chance a terrifying street walker, alone in the pitch black?

*Maybe I should have a psych evaluation at this point.* She sighed and crept closer to slow moving figure, fighting the wind and sleet, making sure to maintain a safe distance.

The figure ahead seemed to sway with the wind, it was almost poetic the way the person moved. Drifting and dancing with the leaves. Entangled in a waltz with the blustery weather, as delicate and thin as a twig.

But after a moment, Tristan started to knit her brows together, and pushed harder on her pedals. Something wasn't right.

The figure was no longer dancing in the wind, but was stumbling, flailing. Looking almost intoxicated.

The drunk drifter appeared to struggle with its legs and motions. Sticking arms out to its sides, as if balancing on a beam in gym. Tristan squinted harder, trying to make sense of what she was watching. Was this even real? What was she looking at?

And suddenly, the figure lost full control of its body, tumbled and hit the ground, landing right in a puddle, no doubt submerged in mud. Movement stopped completely, as if it had lost consciousness on this darkened street, water starting to pound harder on the crumpled form. The darkness was growing deeper and more menacing with every moment.

Tristan shouted out loud, "Hey! Hey! Are you okay?" and stepped harder on her pedals.

She took off straight for the fallen figure. Yelling again, trying to wake the person up with her voice, jumping off her bike and running the last few feet. Sweeping a crumpled friend up in to her arms.

# PART TWO

*Sierra*

# CHAPTER 5

Beep. Beep. Beep. The alarm clock cuts sharply through the sleepy house. Light barely visible through the pull shades to the right of the pillow infested bed, an explosion of greys and whites piled high enough to obscure the small person hidden in the fort.

A thin hand with mauve painted nails reaches out from under a smattering of sheets and blankets, searching pointedly for the alarm clock that slices through the sleepy silence.

Sierra prefers the classic alarm clock to her smudge-free iPhone. It's reliable. It allows her to shut off the bright and endlessly entertaining phone every night before going to bed. If she didn't shut the phone off, she'd scroll through fitness Instagram accounts until dawn broke and painted the sky with peachy streaks. So, a real old school alarm clock aided in focus, kept her in check. And, as an added bonus, the clock was adorable and aided in her bedroom décor aesthetic.

Sierra flipped to her back and pushing the pillow pile to the edge of the high bed. Clearing an area to lay down flat on the mattress and stare at the ceiling, blankly. Sprawling out in the savasana position for a moment, aware that her body is much warmer than her face and neck. Breathing in and out with small burst, her chest rising quick and purposefully. In her meditation she became aware of the rain trickling down the window behind her. Mindful of her heart lightly pumping. Meditation was another activity that kept her grounded. The best part was that there was no wrong way to meditate. Simply feeling was the objective.

How easy it would be to sink back into the welcoming arms of her cushy nest of a bed. Wriggle her body just a few inches lower, cover her face and frame with the swarm of pillows and blankets. Drown to sleep. Sleep she needs. Pushing her responsibilities and stresses aside. Letting the wave of light, airy sleep consume her.

Drifting into the weird place in the mind where you're half awake and half asleep, Sierra began to feel her head slide to the left and the motion of her lolling head jolted her back awake.

Sitting upright finally and taking a deep, steadying breath to soothe and sober her over-used mind, she shook her head to jostle herself awake a bit more. Mentally tricking herself into taking the day by storm, to rally herself into the high energy that her body didn't truly possess. Swinging her legs over to the left side and dangling her feet before plopping onto the cushy carpet. Tightly shutting and widely blinking her eyes, trying to focus and get a grip on the reality she has come to.

Sierra is the first person awake in the whole house, per usual. Her mother would be awake in just about twenty minutes to start getting ready before she would need to rouse the troops.

With three siblings, the house could be relatively chaotic for Sierra's entire family. The only person who didn't have to deal with the insanity daily was her oldest sister Rae.

Rae left the month previously for college. Since leaving, her Snapchat story involved many games of beer pong and Red Bull fueled study sessions at the library.

Other than Rae, Sierra had two younger siblings, as well. Both girls (her poor, but patient father). The younger set of girls were both in middle school. Alex and Anna. Alex was in 8th grade and had just entered the snotty teen stage, Sierra and the rest of the family hoped the phase was short lived.

And Anna played soccer constantly. School teams, private select teams that traveled year-round. This required a lot of their folks' attention and energy. Sierra's mother and father were run ragged, to say the least. There were hushed conversations of, "Oh god, I can't wait until Alex can drive so I can relax a little" regularly when her mother and father cleaned up after dinner.

Since she was the first awake, Sierra took the quiet time to do some in home exercises she found on Instagram and Pinterest. Workouts to help her strengthen her core and flatten her tummy. These were the kind of articles that bombarded her brain at 2am on school nights if she didn't turn her phone off. Sitting in the glow of the phones bright light, she'd pin these motivations to her private board titled, "to do".

Laying on her back and hovering her legs at a ninety-degree angle, the bicycle crunches began. Many of them. She counts to 250 then stops. It only takes a few minutes, but it's enough to calm her shivering mind. And creates an ache in her abdomen.

Flipping to her forearms and midsection floating, while bouncing on her toes, Sierra counts in her head to 100, before dropping to her knees and standing.

Staring into the thick, silver, full length mirror and lifted her oversized sleep t-shirt. Pulling it up high enough so her whole body was visible. From just below her shoulders to her toes, her body was exposed, except for where her boy short underwear from Pink laid. Sierra examined her body. There weren't curves anymore. No squishy bits or baby fat. No warmth. Only peaks and valleys that were bones and slightly developed muscles.

Cringing, she looks away from the malnourished frame that glares back at herself. Shame fills her heart as anxiety floods from her brain, freeing up space to think about how to execute the packed day.

Before continuing with the morning, she flicks through her phone, which was booting up during the workouts. She thumbs through received messages, a few emails, including a newsletter from school about homecoming the following week.

*Great, they have typos. I knew I should have proof read the email.*

Sighing she navigated to the text messages and studied each name and note before quickly responding to everyone with precision.

Making it into her bathroom, which luckily, wasn't shared with anymore. Since Rae left, the door on the other side of the jack-and-jill bathroom never opened. There were no more morning intrusions of privacy or messy sinks coated in crusty tooth paste.

Sierra enjoyed the peace and quiet. Rae could be quite boisterous and always picked on Sierra for being too serious. Sierra thought about Rae while washing her face. Moving slowly, daintily and solemnly. Then applying a light layer of makeup and moving on to methodically getting dressed. She slips into new size zero, high waisted jeans that look fresh out of Nylon Magazine. The inspiration for the jeans and look was the Haim sisters, an indie alternative sister band.

Smiling, and tossing her distressed denim jacket on over the tight, tucked -in, striped turtle neck, she sauntered to her desk to look through her trusty planner.

Sierra is the ASB President. Meaning, she is trying to go to college. She oversees all dances, fundraisers, events and ultimately, the prom and graduation, too.

The pressure is great, especially alongside yearbook and journalism classes, but she balances it all for the sake of the future. The entire student body hopes for and expects good programs and events, and delivering that, is extremely important to Sierra.

Meticulous organization has become a necessity, an obsession even. It's a joke to family and friends. They tease that she schedules her bathroom breaks and can't function without a clock keeping track of every minute. While, this isn't untrue, Sierra doesn't appreciate the lack of support in her organization skills.

The planner is packed to the brim with notes, outlines for the day, and a timeline for ASB's after school meeting. Life is one big calendar. Even when she delegates, she prints out a sheet for the person who is taking over the task and never forgets to check in with them on it.

*Except for that damn newsletter. How did I drop the ball on that?*

The anxiety of a failed project weighs on her. She isn't crazy, but she is very particular. It makes her best friend a little crazy, so Sierra has mentally prepared herself for approximately *one* night a week that is to be dedicated to completely relaxing, kicking back and hanging out. Tristan, her best friend, thinks it's spontaneous, but little does she know, Sierra has it set aside as a spot on her calendar. She just manipulates its time weekly.

Tristan is probably the only person who could get Sierra to bend her schedule. And mainly because Tristan was not only Sierra's best friend and her biggest supporter, but Tristan was also Sierra's hero. Not that she'd ever admit it. She was a free spirit. Nothing ever crushed her or made her feel small. Sierra envied that, and that attitude was something she appreciated being around, even if she couldn't make herself be relaxed in such a way.

The time was running out before she needed to leave for school. So, Sierra filled her leather, crossbody bookbag with the oozing planner and binders. Then skipped towards the kitchen below, but not before giving herself the once over in the full-body mirror one more time, adDannyg the top and scrunching her curls lightly, then exiting.

The kitchen smelled like coffee, freshly printed paper and toast. Her mother stood at the large marble island, laptop propped open and a massive cup of coffee perched on the edge. Her left hand tangled in the dark curly hair perched atop her head, with a pinched look on her face as she scanned emails. Sierra got her hair from her mama.

"Morning, hon! Early ASB meeting this morning?" she glances up from her phone, no doubt checking her emails, "Christ, there are so many emails in my inbox".

"No, just wanting to go sit in the work room to get some things filed and squared away before class" she responds coolly, as she gazes into the fridge. Snacks, lunches, yogurt, fruit, leftover pizza, all the most delicious things stare back at her. Her stomach gurgles slightly, on cue.

Mrs. Simons closes her laptop and sets the coffee down and gives Sierra a long calculating look.

"Sierra, you're looking a bit rough around the edges. Getting enough sleep? Want me to make breakfast?" and she makes a move to grab the egg carton over Sierra's head.

"NO," she says a little too abruptly, as her stomach gives a desperate lurch "Mom. Sorry. No, there are doughnuts in the ASB lounge that I should polish off. Plus, I wanted to use my Starbucks gift card before heading to school, so I'm good. And sleep, yeah. Been keeping my phone off at night. It keeps me from being restless. Good habit, really."

"Oh, good. Well, have a good day sweetie. I'm going to go wake the monsters. Wish me luck. I'll see you for dinner? I'll probably order something, your father and I have some deadlines to make, and by the looks of it, more emails than I know what to do with" she says with a slight chuckle and a quick crazed face while pulling at her locks. Then makes her way out of the kitchen.

"Yup, sounds good. Love you!" Sierra finishes and swirls out of the kitchen. Avoiding the snacks, and fizzy drinks as she goes.

She often catches a ride to school with her neighbor Jay, who is ASB Secretary. And, one of her oldest friends. They grew up across the street from each other, and thus way too comfortable together. Almost sibling like, and Sierra loved that. Plus, Jay had great fashion sense, so he usually applauded her efforts at style, which always made her beam. She got a bit sassier around him.

As soon as stepping out of the door, she sees him walking down his front porch, pulling at his hat in the rain. Sprinting across the lawn she begins to shout at him.

"Lookin' fuckin' snazzy, miss thang" she exclaims. She swore infrequently, but Jay loved when she did. He said it was so unlike her, so she made a point to do it around him because it made him laugh.

She smiles quickly and gestures towards the car, "How's your morning?"

"Ugh, fine. I'm tired as hell though. I don't know how you do all of this! You're so damn organized, and you somehow still manage to look like a goddess for school every morning!"

"Oh, gosh. Don't even," she said, but this was exactly the good morning response she wanted, "You have no idea. Either way, let's get going. I've got some stuff to file before class starts" she says as they both slide into his little two door Honda Civic and gently drift down the cul-de-sac and head to school.

Sierra says goodbye to Jay quickly when they get to school, and she takes off for the ASB lounge, leaving him throwing his arms up in confusion and stomping through the rain on his own. Hustling through the school toward her destination.

Lounge wasn't really a great word for it. It was more a small classroom space, with no windows, lots of cupboards for the junk and paints ASB needed and a small circular table to work at.

A lot of students in ASB used it as a study space, a hideout for when they wanted to skip class or just a place to eat free snacks in the middle of the day. Plus, there was a chalkboard wall, which was fun to doodle on or leave silly messages.

They called it a lounge because last year they used some money from the budget to buy a bunch of twinkly lights and a few floor cushions, Jay's mom donated their old leather couch, so the space was quite cozy now. A home away from home for Sierra. Especially when it was empty.

She hadn't been lying about the doughnuts in the lounge, but she did lie about wanting to eat them. Daniel, the ASB Secretary had brought them in for an evening treat, since the ASB staff stayed late the previous day, and because he had a part time job at the local doughnut shop, Daisy's Donuts and Brew. The brew was an ambiguous joke because sometimes Daisy, the owner, would slip a beer to the truck drivers who stopped through with a wink.

When offered a doughnut the previous day, Sierra had come up with some random excuse that poured out of her mouth before she had time to even process the question. Assumedly, no one noticed. Why would they notice her lack of snacking? Everyone was too busy paying attention to their own selves.

Finishing up the chores before class, her longing eyes lingered on the pink, cardboard box. It's lid slightly ajar. The soft, sickeningly sweet scent dribbled out, dousing the air with a creamy, stomach ache inducing sugary-ness. Flipping open the thick carboard box, she stuck her face close to the doughy, bumpy, middle-less circles. Letting her eyes close, she smelled them. Breathing in their scent, she wafted so heavily she was afraid she might pick up a sprinkle, but instead of making a grab for one of the devious breakfast devils, she slammed the box shut, right as the first bell sounded and swung her bag over her shoulder for the second time that morning.

Taking a deep breath and wishing for time alone for more crunches on the floor of the dirty ASB Lounge. Instead she let herself out of the room and stalked through the hallways to first period.

Smiling at fellow students and responding to the scattered salutations she received. Brown, curly ringlets bouncing happily around her slim, gaunt face. Smiling, smiling all the way.

# CHAPTER 6

Sierra spent the better part of her morning classes scrawling to do lists on the margins of notebooks, half listening to lessons while her brain raced in all directions. The controlling and intellectual tendencies seemed to invade daily life and she couldn't switch it off.

There was always another thing to add to the to do list. There was always something else that could help with a task. She found ways to keep busy, she couldn't breathe without knowing what would happen after the exhale.

Mrs. Simons had, in the previous school year, suggested Sierra go to a therapist. Sierra refused to see how that could be of value and couldn't see how it could fit into her schedule. Rae had joked about Sierra needing anxiety medication, to control the impulsive control issues that emerged and lingered in every little task she completed.

These accusations made Sierra angry, she would storm off during these conversations, refusing to acknowledge that there may be a deeper issue.

It was insulting for anyone to suggest that she needed help, when she was the one who helped everyone else.

And because of all of this, Sierra thrived in leadership roles. Wanting to do things quickly, with accuracy and put a personal touch on every little thing. If it was done her way, then it would, certainly, be done right.

It was all a good way to distract herself from the real problem at hand. Craving the distraction so that the physical cravings in her stomach wouldn't surface as loudly. Groaning and drawing attention.

Throughout the morning; her hand shot up a few times in classes. Partly to answer the questions, but also as a reminder to herself to stay in the present. Letting her mind drift too far down the rabbit hole would put her in a bad place. Visions of burgers and bagels would creep into her brain, which would prompt her to count the calories consumed that week instead of finishing the math assignments.

When the bell finally rang to signal the arrival of lunch time, most of her classmates leapt up, stuffing their bags with their supplies and sprinted for the door. A lot of them were simply in search of a good lunch table, but Sierra knew Tristan had already reserved them a seat since she was one of the kids who would make it their life mission to have a seat by the big windows in the lunchroom, the prime spot.

Slowly rising and emitting a sigh to herself, she carefully gathered her belongings and placed them carefully in the sleek leather bag. She nodded and smiled thoughtfully at her teacher as she left the class.

"See you Monday Ms. Malone, have a good weekend!" she sang with a cheerful smile that was plastered upon her pretty face. Fake but believable.

"You betcha, kiddo! Make it a relaxing one!" she beamed back, wiping down the whiteboard, erasing all evidence of the pre-calculus lesson. Ms. Malone hummed absently and smiled up at Sierra as she departed.

The door shut with a quiet click behind her, she strolled to the lunch room, peering around at the tables. Tristan was bouncing on her toes in line at the snack window for, no doubt, some weird concoction of foods that she would combine and dip into nacho cheese and shove into her unassuming, makeup free face.

Sierra felt a pang of hunger and jealously, as Tristan galloped over to their saved table, where the forest green backpack Tristan carried was flung haphazardly onto the table near the windows. Rain continuing to tap and trickle lightly.

Plopping down into the large squared off plastic chairs, Sierra tucked one leg under the other and unpacked her bag. Producing spiral notebooks, arrow post-it notes, call lists, homecoming ticket mock ups and so on.

Tristan finally arrived at the table, still dancing a bit, with a sideways grin. Shuffling her shoulders with food tottering in her hands and a soda tucked under her arm.

"Hola, my friend" she practically shouted with a smile as she let her smattering of foods tumble onto the table.

"Hey, how's it going?" Sierra responded weakly but with genuine amusement.

"Gooooodddddddd, just had a wildly *boring* morning spent in all of my classes. Except for Ashburn's, of course. And now here I am. How you do? What is all of this?" she gestured at the materials and homecoming items spread out neatly on the table.

Sierra raised an eyebrow and gritted her teeth in a mock, "I've been caught" face.

"No. No, dude, you can't do this at lunch. C'mon. This is crazy! You're going to go insane." Tristan exclaimed as she tossed a bit of soft pretzel into her ajar mouth but giving her best friend a serious look with a tilt of her head.

"T, don't worry! I'm working on the homecoming dance, only. No other projects, I promise. It needs to get done. I know you know it's next weekend I'm just reviewing my details. We have the big meeting tonight" Sierra responded, trying to calm her.

Tristan, being a supportive friend, agreed to let it slide through a mouthful of squishy food that she washed down with a diet coke. Sierra only half understood what she said, but she understood the gist. Tristan wanted to have a relaxing movie night after the dance was over. Sierra made a mental note to put that in her planner and make some time for it.

"Alright" she glared, "Oh! Also, Simon and Co., might wanna hang during slash after homecoming. Maybe we can join forces"

"Sounds good. They're fun guys, but I'm not smoking with them, just so you know" Sierra responded as she turned her attention back to the itinerary in front of her.

"Yeah, yeah. No fun for you, I already know" Tristan joked, "No problem, it'll be fun though. For sure".

Sierra asked Tristan to tell her more about the auditions she had decided to try out for. Mr. Ashburn was running the theater department with a few other faculty members. Tristan thought it would be a great way to hang out with her crush more. They both knew it was silly, but Sierra wanted Tristan to do the musical because she was a talented singer and part of Sierra wanted Tristan to have an activity besides riding her bike and looking for a part time job to keep her busy. Then maybe she'd be able to get into college. And hopefully a school near Sierra.

Tristan spent the better part of the lunch hour chattering away. They didn't have classes together, so this was their only time to catch up during the weekdays, especially with Sierra being so busy with ASB. Sierra listened, smiled, and continued to organize and collect her notes, all the while, her stomach hummed angrily at her. The lively chatter from her friend was a great distraction for Sierra.

A few minutes before the bell is scheduled to sound, signaling the end of lunch, Jay appears at the table. In tow was one of his best gal pals, Becca. They had become inseparable in sophomore year, when they discovered they had plenty of shared interests. They shopped, liked to gossip and watch lots of reality television together. Even though he was still close with Sierra, she didn't really share the same hobbies. So, Jay had taken to finding a good friend in Becca. She was bubbly, quite funny and stood out like a sore thumb. Literally. Her hair was bright blue, and her tight t-shirts usually exposed her rather large bust.

"Hey babe" Tristan says puckering at him followed by a grin.

He waved lightly by wiggling his fingers before hugging her from behind and squeezing her hard. She grinned and glanced up at him.

"We still good for the meeting after school?" he asked, "I want to make sure I'm mentally prepared for a Friday night spent at school..."

"Yup, meet in the ASB room, like ten minutes after classes end? We can make all the posters and get the tickets all organized for the dance. I think I have almost everything else organized! It'll be fun. I think Mr. G is ordering pizza for us too, so even better" Sierra replied.

"Sweet! At least the pizza makes up for some of this painfully uneventful evening. See ya after school then, don't work too hard, love" he said rolling his eyes. She smacked his arm and he winked before wandering away.

"Also, I love those jeans on you, Sierra" Becca spouted, "I wish I was thin enough to pull off high waisted jeans without my hips looking weird! Jealous!"

Sierra blushed, and awkwardly muttered a thank you as they walked away, with Jay pulling Becca in close for a hushed conversation, probably gossiping about the newest of the Hillvale High news.

She appreciated the compliment, she really did, but she didn't want to draw attention to anything.

The bell buzzed faintly, and multiple kids glanced at their phones to confirm the time, grunting with disappointment when they realized the bell had, in fact, been accurate. Just like every other day. Grimaces littered the faces of many students, especially because Friday's always seemed to drag on longer than normal. Tristan started to crumple up her wrappers and stuck her cell phone in her back pocket of her jeans, as she licked her fingers clean of Sun Chip residue.

"Alright, well shit. Lunch is over! Back to reality" Tristan picked her bag up off the floor and leaned over to toss her garbage in the bin behind her.

"Yup, see you later?"

"Sure thing. And hey, did you eat?" she rustled around in her bag, her hand emerging with a granola bar. "Here, take this at least! I think it's chocolate, it'll hold you over until your pizza extravaganza after school". She said with a wink and started to back away towards her next class.

"Yeah, awesome. Thanks." Sierra trailed off, giving Tristan a thumbs-up. And once again started to pack up her entire life into her leather bag

Her next class was as a teacher's assistant for her ASB teacher, so she usually arrived a few minutes late since she could get away with it by feigning a relevant ASB excuse.

She let the lunch room clear out and as soon as she

was alone, began quickly unwrapping the sticky granola bar. Sierra stared at it for a few moments before taking a bite. It was delicious. She chewed and chewed, savoring every single flavor, loving how it stuck to the top of her mouth a bit, but tasted like pure sugar. She walked slowly in the direction of Mr. G's classroom. Chewing and chewing, but purposefully not swallowing.

As she walked, she came to one of the large black garbage cans at the edge of the lunch room. A few more moments of chewing and sticking the glob of sugary oats into the corner of her cheek. Savoring the flavor for a few moments, as her stomach grumbles in anguish and pleading with her to swallow the sustenance.

Finally, she leans over the can and spits the entire ball of mushed food out. Emptying her mouth of the traitorous goodness. She looked at the chewed wad of food, as it sat, perched atop the bundles of food cannisters, wrappers and napkins. Licking her lips and taking a swig of water from her bottle, held loosely in one hand.

The yearning to go to the ASB room and do more sit-ups intruded into the forefront of her mind, which she pushed away, and went to take the stairs up to Mr. G's classroom, counting the stairs as she ascended.

# CHAPTER 7

The wind picked up and the sky started to drizzle again as the school day ended. Sierra continued her usual path through the day. Filled with raised hands, planners being jotted in, assignments being perfectly articulated and other students being both annoyed and impressed with her.

She didn't much mind what the other students thought of her work ethic, she knew they would appreciate her after the school year. She had big plans, was working on the best homecoming and couldn't wait to keep wowing everyone.

She was popular, by the most conventional meaning of the word. She had a lot of people who knew her (obviously, since they voted her to be school president as a Junior. Usually a Senior got this job), she got along well with others and was generally easy to talk to. So, when the bell finally rang to signal the end of the Friday school day, tons of classmates waved at her as she walked through the halls.

"See ya, Sierra! Buying dance tickets now!" a girl

blurted as she nodded and walked passed.

"Looking forward to homecoming, Sierra. Can't wait to see what you got fo' us!" a football player said as he gave her a head nod and a smile.

She smiled at everyone, confidently responded and vivaciously flirted when she got this attention. She was a good sport, and kept her head high, even when her under eyes felt like they were drooping to the floor, her hair was limp and thinning and her belly button felt like it could touch her spine. She consciously touches her stomach over her high waisted jeans and continued making for the hallway that housed her locker.

It didn't take long for Sierra to find Tristan hyperactively bouncing down the hall, and Sierra couldn't help but smirk to herself. She was happy to see someone with such genuine joy.

"Hey, hey!" Tristan exclaimed.

"What have you got, fifteen minutes?" Sierra says.

"Yeah, just about. Wanted to dump these books in my locker and was gonna head to the arts wing after, try to sit with some people that we know. You? Ten minutes, yeah?"

"Yeah, exactly. Then heading to this ASB meeting and then going to call it an early night, but I'm down to hang out this weekend!"

"I'm game. Let's chat this evening?" Tristan responded, as she stuck two thumbs up and wiggles them up and down, looking like she was playing an classic game boy. "I'll catch ya later. Have fun tonight!"

"Good luck!" Sierra shouted over the crowd, as Tristan scampered off, she turned her head looking over her shoulder and smiled back obnoxiously.

Sierra power walked to the ASB lounge, where she knew she would find the crew. She wanted to beat everyone else there, so she could get everything organized and get a spot at the table, not the floor. Blech, the floor was always covered in bit of dust and gum wrappers. Not something to crouch in new jeans, unless absolutely necessary. Like if crunches were needed.

When she arrived, the door was already flung open and Mr. G was inside, rustling around.

"Sierra! Do me a favor, will ya?" he said in his jolly and exuberant tone, barely even looking up.

"Hey, yeah. Of course, what's up?"

"Can you run up to the main office, the pizza delivery kid just called, he said he would leave them up in the office, six pizzas. You can carry that, right? I've already got a bunch of 2 liters down here" he said as he held up a ripping plastic bag with a fizzy orange soda hanging out and plastic cups.

"Right. Yeah, on it" she said, feeling defeated, and brought her hand to her stomach again. Setting her bag down and then hitting the halls once again.

In the office, the secretary gestured for the corner of the far counter, as she was still on the phone, and mouthed, "those are for you".

Sierra mouthed back, "Thank you" with a smile and slid the massive pizzas into her thin arms, tottering slightly.

Stumbling her way down the hall, barely able to see over the stack of boxes. The lovely scent of melted cheese, pepperoni's and crunchy crust wafted into her nose, as her arms got damp from the bottom of the sweaty, greasy pizzas. Her mouth watered, and stomach groaned with desire. She found herself blushing as she trudged down the hall under the weight of the food. The ASB lounge finally came into view, she tried to lighten her mood and goofily hollered, "Delivery! Coming through!" and raised her eyebrows with a silly face as she entered.

A few people clapped while she curtsied and laughed, and Jay snatched the boxes out of her arms, giving her some relief. He set them strategically on the table.

*So much for working on the table*, she thought.

"Dig on in people! Feast!" Mr. G exclaimed.

The whole ASB team started a cramped line, with Jay at

the front, leading the hungry pack.

Sierra hung back.

*Maybe if I look busy getting my stuff out, no one will notice I'm not in line and the pizza will run out.*

The line finally cleared, and Sierra found a spot on the floor with Jay. After all, today was poster day. The group had to paint all the posters that would be put up around school to advertise the homecoming dance. A few groups were painting other signage that would be used during the homecoming game. Everyone had a different poster style. Some were banners, some squares. Other kids were sorting through the tickets and props, while others updated the Student Life page on the website with the remaining details for the homecoming dance for the coming week.

"Sierra, come fill up! You didn't get in line and I *won't* be taking any pizza home" Mr. G said with a grin on his face, patting his belly.

"Oh. Right, okay. Sorry, I got distracted" she responded guiltily with an internal cringe.

She stood up and brushed her hands on a paper towel. Approaching the table, snagged a paper plate and stared into the face of the food. Without thinking, began piling three large pieces high on to her plate.

Sitting back down, she took a swig of water and started

to inhale the food.

Her stomach taking over her brain. It took everything in her conscious being to not moan with every bite she took, she was filled with what she imagined was close to pure ecstasy. Closing her eyes and diving in, savoring every single moment. Felt her mouth fill with unhealthy, tasty, glorious pizza-y goodness. Her brain was happy, face felt full, heart sang, and stomach bloated.

One. Closing her eyes and inhaling the savory scent, munching loudly. Two. Tearing the crust apart and dipping it savagely into the pile of ranch dressing on Jay's nearby plate. Three. Big, painful swallow and a deep breath. Her stomach expanded, her jeans felt tight and she still hadn't chugged any liquids.

Even though Jay was talking the whole time she ate, when Sierra finally delved back into reality, she noticed that Jay had been watching her.

"Damn girl. You just vacuumed those up!" he smiled quickly, trying to erase his enthusiasm at seeing her slurp up a pile of greasy food.

"Language, Jay" Mr. G distractedly hollered as he typed away at his computer, not looking up.

"Damn isn't a swear word! But really Sierra. You wolfed that down. Love it!" he laughed and looked at her approvingly.

Sierra giggled with embarrassment and felt shame. Her mind shouted, told her she was dumb, she ruined all that hard work, she felt the urge to go on a run. She hated herself. She wanted to maintain her shape, control her cravings, and she just failed. She felt absolutely ruined by her gluttonous act. Mind racing, and panic ensued.

"Mr. G, I'm going to run back to the office, make some confirmation calls with the DJ and photographer! The cell service down here sucks" she said, looking at him for approval.

"Yes, good idea. Come back quick though, I think we are wrapping up soon" Mr. G responded, finally looking up over his laptop.

Sierra swept up her planner. She had all the contacts in her planner for the dance. But she had already confirmed with them yesterday. The idea of a few moments of solace sparked the escape. Alone with her thoughts and disappointments.

She speed walked around the corner and up a flight of steps, in the direction of the main office, but a few doors down is a private bathroom. Where solace and alone time was possible. And no one ever used it.

A bunch of the lights in the school are off by then, and

the main office's light were turned low, so Sierra knew she wouldn't be disturbed. She stomped quicker as she neared closer to the door. Stinging tears building in the corners of her eyes.

She flings the door open, flicks on the light as she turns the door to locked and drops her planner on the floor with a loud slap. Sweeping her hair in one fell motion into a loose pony tail at the nape of her neck, squatting down to her knees in a huff and, immediately sliding the ring and middle fingers of her right hand into her mouth. Grasping desperately for the uvula to enact her gag reflex.

The familiar sensation welcomed her. Hot bile and chunks of food rush into her mouth and she loudly vomits her entire meal into the clean school toilet.

*Rinse and Repeat* she said to herself. And repeated three or four times. Until there was nothing left to evacuate from her body, until all that was left was clear mucus.

*Was that really better? Do you really feel better now?*

She takes three deep, meditative breaths and stands up. Flushing the toilet, sending her vomit and her shame down the drain.

Taking a paper towel from the dispenser and dabbing at the corners of her eyes. Then gulping water from the faucet and gurgling the water, attempting to rid herself of the taste of barf and pepperoni's.

Finally, smoothing her jeans out, she pulls her top down and yanks the hair tie out of her curly hair, letting her dull hair fall loosely to frame her gaunt face once more.

Taking a moment to examine herself in the mirror, wishing for a piece of gum and seeing her collar bones popping out dramatically from underneath her turtleneck. Even something modest couldn't hide the evidence of her secret.

As she tosses her paper towel into the small mounted silver garbage can, she hears angry footsteps approaching. Suddenly fear floods her system. Was she caught? Was she in trouble? Hurriedly unlocking the door, flicking off the light and slipping out of the bathroom and down the nearest darkened hall before the angry, stomping person caught up with her.

She peered around the corner, to see where the person went. Her eyes land on a furious looking Lyss Rogers, drama kid extraordinaire flying down the hall. Red faced, crying and tightly squeezed fists barging around the corner, swinging open the single bathroom and disappearing inside. She shouted a few expletives and went quiet.

Sierra took this as her chance to run back to the ASB group. Going back the other way and slipped back into the group discussion. She confirmed with everyone they were confirmed with all the hired contractors for the dance.

"Alright, all confirmed! Photos and DJ are a go!" she smiled. Jay gave her a concerned looking, side-eye.

# CHAPTER 8

Mr. G looks up from his laptop and glances at his watch. "Whoa kids. It's got to be getting dark, it's also Friday. What are all of you still doing here? Shouldn't you be at the movies with friends? Or causing trouble somewhere?" he jokes, "Time to get out of here. I think we are MORE than prepared".

Everyone starts to pack up, stick things away, pile up posters.

"Sierra. Want a ride? Or is your mom coming for you today?" Jay asks, as he rinses off his paint brush, looking a little bit apprehensive.

"Oh! Mom's coming, thanks. Family dinner, so we're grocery shopping I think. Catch ya this weekend?"

"Sure, I'll see ya soon!" he says, and Sierra wanders out the door.

Her mom isn't coming to pick her up, she simply wants more time alone, time to reflect and scroll through her phone. Burn some calories, take in the cold air and listen to music. She fumbles in her backpack for her delicately folded up ear buds and plugs them into her phone as she opens Spotify on her phone. *30% battery, perfect for the 20-minute walk home.*

Shifting her book bag over her slim shoulder, she buttons her oversized denim jacket, pulls a beanie over her thick curls and steps out the side exit of the school. Starting to walk home. The night covering her and her path.

The brisk evening feels good on her face. She scrunches her shoulders up to her ears to keep the heat close to her face. The wind howls in the bushes and trees that line the sidewalk.

*Oh, it's much cooler than I thought.*

She glances at her weather app, it's still 47 degrees...not too cold.

*Why am I so flipping cold?*

She stuffs her hands further into her jean jacket and shivers a bit but puts the cold out of mind as she watches the houses and buildings that she slowly passes.

*There are people inside of those houses. Warming up, making dinner, planning movie nights. Tucking their young kids in bed, being happy.*

This makes her smile a bit. Warms her heart, but

unfortunately not her body. A few rain droplets fall on the bridge of her nose, she looks up and sees the streaks of rain fall more incessantly. Rain comes down a bit faster, not a full shower, but more than a mist.

Speeding up the pace of her legs and thinking about her mom, who would be mad that she didn't call for a ride if she gets home and is completely soaked. She turns her head to the right to watch a car fly by. The movement makes her eyes blur. Or perhaps she got a raindrop in her eye. It throws her off, a bit. Sierra scrunches her face up, frustrated that she'll need to pull her hands out of her warm pockets.

She reaches up to her eyes, to poke the rain droplet out of her line of site. But the action does nothing, her vision in both eyes has started to blur, as if she pulled off a pair of glasses that she doesn't use.

Concerned she rubs more rigorously, her cold fingers barely moving, and blinks furiously.

*What? Why is it so hard to see? I don't understand. I feel so dizzy.*

Beginning to slow to almost a stop, shaking her head left to right, trying to clear her vision. The quick motions only make her feel dizzier, and she begins to take a few steps on the sidewalk, trying to right herself. Her head starts to loll on her neck as she tries to steady herself. Her stomach growls angrily at her, a monster awakening and punishing her for her mistreatment, her sins.

She comes to what she thinks is a standstill and tries to bend her knees, her choir teachers always said locking your knees made you light headed. But she had been moving, hadn't she? She wasn't locking her knees if she was walking. They weren't locked. The trees overheard seemed so menacing now, not the light lovely pieces of nature she usually thought they were.

*Wait, why am I looking up. Looking forward, Sierra, you silly girl. Start walking home. You got this. This must be some anxiety thing.*

Her thoughts started to swirl, as her breathing sped up. Concern was mounting, and the ability to continue trekking home seemed impossible. The clouded mind reminded her of when she had a few glasses of wine at dinner last Thanksgiving, instead of eating the turkey. She had found speech difficult and her brain spun endlessly when she tried to sleep through her giggles.

*Okay, let's look for milestones, like you do when you run. Pick a spot and that's the next destination. Get there and pick a new place until you're home. Or call mom, she's probably home from picking Anna up from soccer training.*

Stumbling to the right a bit, catching her balance and

trying to take a deep breath, but the next jerk to the side had her tottering and finally plummeting to the soft wet ground, her sight black.

The last thing she remembered was hearing a familiar voice shouting before she went numb and let her body go. Embracing the cold and the wet.

# PART THREE

*Simon*

DOWN THE PRIMROSE PATH

# CHAPTER 9

The back of the class was just a little bit warmer than the rest of the room. There was a whirring heat vent right above the back right-hand corner that blasted warm air downward, making the papers on whoever sat underneath its warm, sputtering breath, dance in the artificial breeze.

In this corner lived a desk with a missing foot, so it wobbled crookedly whenever its occupant shifted even slightly in the seat. But Simon, its current inhabitant had perfected the art of balance in this desk. Laying his beanie clad head lightly on the center of the surface, left arm tucked in tightly to his abdomen, while his left arm cupped around the crown of his head. A small cave made for the laziest of morning people.

Simon Matthews wore black skinny jeans, with a hole starting to form in the knee of his left leg, a baggy black hoodie zipped to the top, and had a navy-blue beanie pushed low on his head, covering his medium length, choppy hair.

He was thin, tall, with freckles sprinkled across the bridge of his nose and cheeks.

Today, a wave of exhaustion had washed him away, taking him as a casualty. He was usually tired, staying up late, writing, watching movies and watching the lights in his neighbors' houses plinking out slowly, while his lamp blazed on, becoming too warm as the night wore on.

He kept the lights low in the tiny, shabby bedroom and sat at the rickety desk, laptop shooting streaks of colors and movement out at him, while he hunched over and scribbled away on loose leaf paper. Propping open the window every so often, to blow the smoke from his cigarette's or spliffs out the window. Then he'd spray an aerosol air freshener can with gusto until the room was not only fresh but also slightly damp. A new damp haze overtaking the original smoky cloud.

The act of drifting to sleep didn't usually happen until well after two in the morning, sliding into bed and dozing off for a few hours until he had to wake up to get to school. The incessant phone alarm screaming at him at 6:45 on the dot. Enough time for him to scrounge a pair of clean pants out of the dryer and shove his favorite, label-less beanie over his hair, mashing it into his eyes. Simon regularly shit talked his school, but one good thing could be found in their lax dress code. Hats were 100% allowed in class and it saved Simon in a pinch more than once.

This morning, he rode his bike to school. Sometimes Logan would pick him up, but today Simon just rolled out of his flannelled bed and hopped on his slightly rusty bike. Backpack bobbing on his back as he lazily pedaled in the misty morning to the high school, he didn't want to be a burden on Logan every day. The cold air woke him up slightly, but as soon as he were to sit under the heater in first period, he'd drift into a sleepy stupor again.

Shortly after arriving and halfheartedly sucking on a cigarette by a side entrance of the school for a few minutes before abandoning about three quarters, he let it fall to the ground and rubbed his foot on it until it was shredded. He wandered into the school, to snag a cup of coffee and go catch a few minutes of shut eye before class.

The thing about Simon was he wore this tired, dingy look well. His smirk was swoon worthy, and after his first classes, he'd usually perk up. But sleepiness never destroyed the humor.

Fast forward: here he sat. The bell about to ring in Mr. Ashburn's class, notebooks already strewn out on the desk he occupied, back warming from the push of warm air. He began to stir as more students poured into the class, discussing their boring lives like it was a romantic comedy or sitcom.

Simon disliked and sarcastically mocked many of his classmates. His distain emerged when he, at a young age, realized that his folks were outliers in the community.

Neither of his parents had great jobs, neither made much money. And his parents spent a lot of money on the healthcare of his mother's parents. Grandpa was mentally deteriorating, and Grandma was a mess about it, unable to afford or look for solutions. So, a large portion of the meager paychecks went right to taking care of the extended family. Which didn't leave much left over for Simon and his siblings. Simon had a lot less than his peers. In a community like Hillvale, most were privileged beyond their understanding and somehow, his family had settled in this area, which was beyond Simon's understanding.

This fact often caught up with him. He was a lively guy, but his kryptonite was rich assholes with an agenda. Hillvale High had no shortage of these characters.

The class was nearly full, and Simon listened to the girl next to him complain about how her car didn't have enough space, and how she wished she had got to pick her own car when she turned sixteen.

Simon smiled to himself and rolled his eyes as he sat up in his chair as though rising from the dead. Plastering an ironic smirk to his dewy face.

He grunted and made a big show about stretching and yawning loudly, which consisted of a very loud yell as he exhaled the yawn. The girls next to him stared through the corner of their eyes, eye rolls on the cusp of happening, their conversation completely halted by his obnoxious intrusion. His eyes finally settled on them, a sly smile stretched across his lips.

"Must be real tough being you, not enough space for what? Your tennis rackets and ego?" he said, sarcasm and an edge evident in his tone.

"You're a dick, Simon" the blonde one spat back and flicked her blown out hair behind her shoulder and turned to face the front of the room as the bell rang, obviously miffed by his comment.

Simon chortled to himself as he put his feet on the back of Tristan's seat in front of him and pushed lightly on it, so that she bounced a bit and her hair started to sway. Sticking his lower jaw out in mock aggression, which went unnoticed.

Tristan was completely out of it, staring lightly out the window at the rain and the falling leaves. So, he kept his feet on the back of her chair but stopped pushing. Thinking she'd spin around and stick her tongue out at him soon, but she was fully disengaged from reality. Simon noticed she did this a lot and shook his head at the back of her long hair, sleepy smile still engaged. Tristan was one of the biggest goofs he knew, and they were friends because of it.

Mr. A entered the room a moment later and finally Tristan returned to reality. Turning her head to face the front of the room. And swatting at Simon's feet on her chair, making them drop back to the floor.

*She's got a cruuuussshhhhh*, Simon thought, wiggling in his chair and sitting up straighter. Sipping his paper cup of coffee and sugar for the remainder of class.

The rest of the lesson passed by without any effort on Simon's part. He didn't pay much attention to the discussion but did note how most of the girls gave Mr. Ashburn their undivided attention. Something he found both hilarious and confusing.

*I mean, he's a handsome dude, but still. A teacher? Blech, what is this, Pretty Little Liars or some shit? Also, I can't believe I know enough details about that show to make a reference.*

The bell rang after just under an hour later, and Simon tried to shuffle out of the room. But Tristan was blocking the aisle. Quite literally throwing supplies into her stupid green backpack, and unaware of the people around her. Simon knew what was going to happen before it even did, and he stuck his left hand up to block the blow. Tristan went to haphazardly fling her bag over one shoulder, and the straps flung up, smacking Simon on the arm.

He chuckled, because she hardly seemed to realize that she made impact with a solid object.

"Ow!" he mock shouted with a smile, louder than necessary and feigned pain with a hand over his nose, "My nose job! Daddy won't pay for another!"

"Oh!" she spun around with wide eyes, "I'm so sorry Simon, I wasn't paying attention, you alright? Did I really hit your face? I'm so sorry. Jesus. "

"All good, Miss Scatterbrain!" he smirked, placing a hand on her shoulder and shaking her a bit, "Have a good rest of your day, I hope you get more chances to fawn over Mr. A", he batted his eyes quickly and clasped his fists together at his heart.

She turned red briefly under her curtain of blonde beach waves but smirked as he spun away and out the door with a flourish.

Simon moseyed down the hall, with his hands tucked into his front pockets. He gave a head nod to a few people in the hall, keeping an eye out for Logan. They usually didn't run into each other until lunch, but he hadn't heard from Logan that morning, so he wasn't sure if he got to school on time anyway. He also kept his eyes peeled just in case he had the chance to run into Lyss Rogers.

He'd happily bump her lightly, slide her a wink and quick grin while smoothly landing a joke. But lady luck wasn't on his side that morning. Slipping into his next class, he quickly swept up a seat in the back again and scribbled in the margins of his papers. Avoiding conversations with his peers and trying to focus on anything *but* the homecoming dance; the primary hushed conversation topic of the day, apparently.

# CHAPTER 10

Simon rolls through the day at an immensely slow pace. *Sometimes these slow days make me feel more stoned than when I'm actually stoned.*

It's Friday, the rain outside continues dripping lightly and consistently outside, creating puddles, and darkening clouds rolling across the sky, threatening heavy showers. A majority of the student body is ready to depart for the weekend.

Supposedly, Moe, a friend of Logan and Simon's, was throwing a party that weekend. His parental units were in France. His male gamete donor had some important job that required incessant travel, and Moe's female gamete donor usually tagged along for long weekends of pampering and mimosas. The event was a pre-homecoming weekend get-together. A handful of people were invited, and undoubtedly more than the invited crew would make an appearance. The soiree would be an interesting event and Simon crossed his fingers that Lyss was going, and hopefully sans Derek.

Derek was a meat head character. He had become Lyss' shadow the previous school year, courting her even through her pained and unamused expressions. Derek referred to Lyss as his girlfriend, but Lyss simply *didn't* refer to Derek. Ever. At least as far as Simon could make out.

Simon and Logan had a pretty vast group of friends, but they were relatively low key. They showed up to parties, drank a bit, and smoked a bit more. They got along with almost everyone. A friendly group of stoners with no real beef and no real opinions. The guys fell into the category of well-liked and non-threatening. Others enjoyed Simon because he was funny and sarcastic, but he was also the group's loose cannon. Most likely to explode. To get in a fight. But, Simon was lucky; his family was big enough where his folks didn't mind what he did on the weekends especially if he wasn't getting into any serious trouble. No cops, no problem.

There was an unspoken deal in the family, "You can do whatever you want until you fuck up".

So, Simon made a point to cause as little trouble as possible. Just toeing the line regularly, a sprinkling of mayhem. A little chaos kept him sane. Simon was pretty quick-to-anger, and he was careful to keep himself in check.

Maintaining freedom and building his own future was

important. Even if school wasn't his priority, he wanted as many options as he could maintain.

When the bell for lunch chimed, like most of the students, he tossed his shit in his backpack and hauled ass out of the door. Quickening his pace to get to the lunchroom quickly. He was on the far end of the school and didn't want to spend the first 10 minutes of the precious lunch half-hour in line getting some cruddy, undercooked snack.

Gliding into the lunch line behind none other than Logan.

"Yo" he said and clucked his tongue.

"Hey man" Logan smiled back at him.

They chatted while in line, Simon's hands tucked into his pockets and Logan playing with his hoodies strings. Pulling them up and down. Left. Right. Up. Down.

Logan ordered a small feast of food at the counter. Per usual, stocking up on a bunch of snacks, instead of a true meal. Craving sugar, carbs, salt. Logan managed to shove most of the food into his pockets and arms and jerked his head to the side, letting Simon know he'd find them a table. Simon nodded back and turned to order.

"Whatcha gettin' sweetheart?" the sweet lunch server smiled. She liked to flirt with Simon. And she was his favorite lunch lady, a charming middle-aged woman that glowed.

"Hey stunner! Let's get me the usual" he said kindly and fumbled in his pockets for change and a few bucks he had left over from buying coffee that morning. He counted the change and she laughed as she jokingly tapped an imaginary watch on her left wrist.

"Here ya go, milady" he said, certain he was short by about fifty cents, but she didn't seem to notice. She swept the change up into her palm and flung it into the register and was already tossing a happy grin at the next student.

He hated that. Always scrambling to have enough cash. His folks weren't exactly great about remembering to give him cash and it's not like there was much to divvy up anyway. With all his siblings and his folks taking care of the grandparents, things were always tight on funds. It was a small miracle he had his own bedroom, as this point. And, even though confidence seeped from his pores, he was hyperaware that he was the only kid he knew who shopped for new clothes at a second-hand store.

He scanned the tables for a moment, while he shoved a handful of sour cream and onion chips into his mouth, crumbs falling to the floor and scattering across his dark sweatshirt. Logan tossed his hand in the air, seeing Simon gazing through the hordes of students.

Simon plops down in the wide, plastic chairs and

scoots in close, so both of his elbows splay out on the table.

"Dude, finally Friday. Thank fuck" Logan says to Simon.

"Yeah, agreed. It's been one hell of a boring day. Just been listening to a lot of complaining," he starts to imitate the girls from first period, "Daddy didn't buy me the right car. It was only 20 thousand dollars instead of 25 thousand. UGH". He rolls his eyes and smirks at Logan.

Logan snickers, "That's so annoying. But, really, it's nothing new is it? This school is full of that bullshit".

Logan's family was doing well, but they were a frugal family, which Simon appreciated. Because even though they had money, they didn't flaunt it. They believed in nice vacations and saving for Logan's education post high school rather than showering him in gifts. Plus, his folks had just divorced, so his mom was careful to spend only as she needed to, his dad was the one in the family who was happy to indulge, but he wasn't around anymore. Logan never talked about it. But, Simon did have to admit that Logan had some great shoes, but his car was kind of a beater. Which was also great because they never felt bad hot boxing it.

"That's true. You think I'd be used to it by now. But the bitter *animal* in me just keeps popping out" Simon replied, "So what do we got cookin' this weekend? There is that party on Saturday at Moe's, you still down?"

"Yeah, that'd be cool. I'm down to do something tonight too, if you just want to chill?" Logan raises his eyebrows in question while polishing off his toxic colored Gatorade.

"Sure thang. That'd be..." Simon trails off as he spots Lyss Rogers. Talking animatedly with her friends and sipping a Diet Coke through a straw.

Logan starts to laugh, noticing the source of the distraction, "You, my friend, are ridiculous. Isn't she supposed to be a total bitch? Like, classic mean girl type?"

"I don't know. I don't think so. I feel like when I've interacted with her before she seemed, like, *ready* to be normal. But then one of her bimbo friends always pops up out of nowhere and she turns into an ice queen again. Maybe we'll see her this weekend". He smirks and shoves some more chips into his mouth and wipes the crumbs on his knee. His fingers linger, feeling the size of the hole that has formed.

"Yeah, she'll probably be there. I heard from Moe. But you know she'll be there with Derek" Logan pointed out.

He was probably right, but from what everyone knew, Derek and Lyss weren't an item and maybe never had been. Simon could swear she rolled her almond eyes at Derek when he wasn't looking.

"That guy is such a douche. And a dick. You see his car?" Simon, spun around in his chair again, turning his point of focus to Lyss completely.

"Dude, quit staring" Logan said, throwing his hands up exasperated, "But yes, I saw the car. It's sweet, but ridiculous".

"I want to catch her eye! Don't ruin my game. And yes, the car is great. I want it. Maybe I'll swipe it" Simon said, throwing a gleaming smile in Logan's direction, who laughed and rolled his eyes.

"Classic weirdo-Simon" he chuckled.

Simon just kept his gaze in her direction for another moment or two, ready to give up. Then she finally glanced over at him and they made quick eye contact, which she held longer than she needed to. He gave her his signature side smile, and stuck his fingers up, as a hello.

She blinked at him and turned away as Derek approached, her shoulder deflating a little at the site of his arrival. If Simon didn't know better, he would have thought she blushed when he looked at her. But hey, it was hard to tell from half way across the cafeteria.

Turning back to his table, a few other friends arrived. They wanted to know what the plans for the weekend were.

They agreed to keep in touch about the party and continued to toss chips and cheese drenched soft pretzels into their mouths.

Simon and Logan wrapped up lunch as the bell rang, signaling the beginning of the end of the school day.

Simon sauntered across the lunch room in the direction of his next class. He could hear some guys behind him, talking.

"Dude, she'll put out" one guy said.

"She's so hot man, and with that new car, you're totally gonna seal the deal".

It was Derek and two of his buddies. Clearly, they were referring to Lyss Rogers.

"I hope so. That fucker is nice and clean, smells nice. Will probably get her all excited. Sure gets me excited!"

They laughed with a chortle only football players could muster.

"And look who we have here" the sadistic voice said, noticing Simon sulking ahead of them. Simon, cringed.

*Dammit. Of course. Almost a whole week without them fucking with me, but they couldn't just steer clear. No doubt I'm in for a materialistic reaming.*

His lack of a car, his clothes and his attitude was often under fire by the jock-type characters at their school. Simon suspected they were jealous of him in some capacity, but it was hard to convince himself of that. Really, what made Simon mad was how ridiculously stereotypical the bullies surrounding him were.

*What is this? An eighties film?*

"Scrawny little Simon! My favorite tiny little impoverished friend. Simon? You still riding your bike to school? If I were you, I'd be scared to ride it, it might fall apart under the weight of the rust!" Derek chortled, and his cronies stifled their grunting laughs.

Attempting to remain calm, Simon kept walking, his face getting warmer.

*Control your anger. Control it. Think about seeing Lyss this weekend. These guys aren't worth the trouble.*

"Oh, quiet today, huh buddy? Well, if you ever need a ride home let me know, there is plenty of room in the trunk".

Derek clearly thought he was a genius in comedy and so did his braindead trust fund baby friends.

*Fuck you. Fuck you. Fuck you. Keep it together, Simon. Keep it together, you're better than this.*

Fists clenched and keeping a tight smile on his face even though inside was a cloud of fumes and rush of ferocity. Derek and his friends, at some point stopped walking and turned into a classroom, but Simon couldn't remember when.

He just kept walking, his face calm as he did a lap around the school, before making his way to class late.

He shook the frustration away and forced himself to be cool and collected.

# CHAPTER 11

The school day came to a miraculous close. Simons mood had lightened, but not subsided quite yet. And the halls of Hillvale High was flooded with teens. A constant roar of voices, high pitched laughter and the slamming of lockers, as students ditched their supplies for the weekend. Car keys jingled, and cell phones buzzed with Twitter notifications and texts. Girls ducked behind screens, pouting their lips for Instagram stories.

With the homecoming dance and game coming up the following week, there was a pronounced buzz about the students. With the event brought spirit week, so everyone would come to school on Monday in pajamas. Then crazy hair, face paint, suspenders and on Friday a sea of green and gold would flutter and cling to bodies and pieces of hair.

Assuming he remembered, Simon would only participate in the last day, where he wore his green and gold sunglasses he spray-painted the previous year. The school pride thing was fun, but he didn't put much effort into dressing up.

Simon joked around with a couple of friends on the way out of school, like many of their peers, they were scheming for the weekend.

Figuring out when they'd get together to have a few beers (and how the hell they'd even get the beer. Jared and Tony had older siblings that could usually hook them up. But it usually required some extra cash that usually ended up in their siblings' pockets) and where they were going to crash for the late evenings. It was usually easiest to slyly slip into Logan's house late at night. His mom had a heart of gold and frequently turned a blind eye on the boys' antics. So, Simon and Logan could come in bleary and red eyed as the sun was rising and she'd still have breakfast warm for them when they finally emerged in the afternoon, after a full mornings rest.

It was still early in the school year, so most students weren't bogged down with homework or projects yet, but everyone was getting ready for when the storm would hit. The whirlwind always seemed to weigh heavily on them two weeks before winter break, which was eyeroll inducing. Which meant, almost everyone was up for some post-summer partying.

With the general plan for Saturday solidified, the fellows started to part ways, shielding themselves from drizzling rain as they dispersed and splashed their way out the main entrance of the school.

Simon hangs back for a few, bouncing on his toes, getting up the courage to make a break for the bike rack. Logan had offered a ride, but the bike wouldn't fit in the trunk. Better to ride it home and be soaked now than later.

Approaching the bike rack, a loud engine revs heavily a few rows away. Followed by chortling and the ground shaking sound of rap music over a heavily bass-y trap tune. Simon lazily lifted his gaze to meet the source of the obnoxious show, ready to be annoyed immediately.

Derek and his squad were sauntering to his new car, the rain barely affecting their shaved heads. Derek's care was a gift from his very rich daddy. A sleek gun metal grey Audi, with large sunroof, sleek wheels and, if anyone questioned it before, they didn't now, a bumping stereo system. The group of buffoons were high fiving and mouthing the words to the degrading lyrics.

Simon glowered in their direction, still pissed about earlier that afternoon.

*That guy is such a dick. Look at him and his buffoons,* Simon thought, agitated, angry and annoyed. He stood supporting the weight of his bike, watching them for a moment longer. He rolled his eyes and went to put his bike lock in his bag.

He kicked a rock, it shook along the sidewalk, and into the parking lot. A second later, the Audi rushed by and someone shouted, "Shit Stain!" at Simon as he mounted his bike. The statement was followed by a steady stream of pompous, bumbling laughter. Simon immediately flung his right leg over his bike and started pedaling like mad, trailing behind the pristine car, splashing water all over his recently washed jeans when he flew through the puddle nearest him.

His brow was beginning to drip with perspiration, his back moistened with every pump of his legs. Sweat and rain were dripping down his back between his skin and his sweatshirt and backpack. He was doing his best to stay caught up with the slick car.

Simon stayed some ways behind Derek, and eventually found himself in one of the more expensive neighborhoods in town after about fifteen minutes of pedaling, his breath now completely ragged and beat.

Pillared homes, whose ceilings were probably eighteen feet tall on each floor. Huge windows that could only be described as extravagant, from floor to ceiling, with lush curtains dangling. Freshly manicured lawns with perfectly pruned shrubs and flowers lining walkways. And, most ridiculously, fountains lazily spewing water into algae infused water basins in the middle of a few half circle driveways, leading to massive garage spaces.

He slowed down, taking in the scenery. Half impressed and half embarrassed. This neighborhood was like a foreign land to him. Everything was beautiful, but ridiculous. Completely unnecessary but it was still quite a sight. He thought about how pretty it must have looked during the holidays when little colored lights were lining the driveways and each edge of the houses meticulously designed corners.

Simon's enjoyment of the stunning neighborhood and signs of excessive living ended quickly. He felt his heart sink to the smooth pavement, leaving a deep ache. These people fill their space and lives with money, toys and materials, but Simon couldn't even pay full price for his school lunch. The middle class tell their kids they can be wealthy and successful with hard work and dedication, but Simon had watched his folks work their asses off, day in and day out without much to show for it. Money was a fairytale to Simon. Payoff for hard work seemed nearly unreal. Sure, some people fell into money (like Derek) but moving up in the world, gaining this level of prestige and status was unbelievable. Simons hatred thudded in his chest, in the hole where his heart had been before it dropped dead on the slick cement under his rusted bike.

*Who spends money on this shit?* he thought to himself, as he drooled over the huge landings and terraced homes. At some point, after a few minutes of gawking, Simon realized he had completely lost Derek and his ride.

Pushing down a few blocks and searching in haste, the rain starting to chill him, goosebumps formed on his forearms. Glancing into each driveway he passed, looking for the grey Audi, hoping that Derek didn't drive into a garage and close it, leaving him completely lost.

Finally, he came across a home with the Audi parked out front. A sprawling chateau, plenty of trees, four garage doors and a circular driveway. A few lights were illuminated inside, one garage door stood open, and inside was another luxury vehicle, with beefy tires and sparkling paint. Simon slipped off his bike, and let it fall to the sopping grass that lined the walkways. He stood in front of the house, staring in awe for a moment, and thinking to himself, wondering what Derek's parents did for a living. Was this a trust fund? Did they have wonderful jobs? Did Derek get to inherit some expansive family business when he was ready?

Simon had no clue. And even though he wondered, he didn't care. All that mattered was Derek was a grade-A asshole and was spoiled rotten. His parents probably showered him in gifts, floated him hundred-dollar bills daily and gave him credit cards with no max. There was no way they even knew their sweet prince of a son was actual a bumbling douche.

The idea of a joy ride in the small sportscar was tempting. Hard to pass up. Trying to convince himself to just leave, he strode closer to the car, rain slapping its hood. He'd be able to recline in leather seats, ass heaters flicked on, the stereo bumping loudly (with real music, not that idiotic rap music Derek liked), a cigarette stuck between the tinted window crack and the painted door frame. He knew he shouldn't even dare, but sometimes.... he just couldn't help himself.

*Who cares? He'll know it was me anyway.*

Simon could see the alarm in the car was on, a small red light blinked on and off on the dash. Glancing at the garage, he stalked up the driveway.

Tiptoeing into the opened garage. He shuddered, scared someone may come flying through the door and see him. Standing still for a moment, listening for any voices or footsteps that may be approaching. All that could be heard were a few deep voices inside, but just barely. Their voices were being covered up the loud pings and bangs that Simon could only guess was a video game. Every few moments, he'd hear someone holler something like, "Oh, YES!".

He took this to mean that he had at least a few safe moments in the garage. Glancing around, he saw ski equipment and two large Rubbermaid bins labeled 'Halloween' sitting on the glossy floor, with the holidays approaching, it looked like Derek's mom was ready to decorate.

*Or maybe his servants are ready to decorate.* He rolled his eyes.

He stepped lightly around the bins toward the few wooden steps that would lead into the house. And there! Gleaming as if a gift from the damn gods, was a small wooden key hanger with two empty pegs, and two pegs with keys dangling innocently.

A smile stretched across Simons face and he slowly reached for the pair that had a Hillvale High School key chain on it, and a small Audi key.

As soon as the item was in his hands, he spun around as fast as possible and sprinted out of the garage, sliding to a stop and fumbling with the key fob, clicking the unlock button.

The headlights flashed briefly. Heart pounding harder than it ever had, he tugged quickly but lightly on the handle. Gritting his teeth, still terrified the alarm might sound.

It didn't. Eyes wide, he ducked his head and plopped down, soaking wet, in the driver's seat.

The interior smelled of copious amounts of cologne and of weed. He stuck the key in the ignition and let the engine purr at him.

Pushing the car into drive and sailing down the driveway, thankful that the car was automatic and not manual transmission. Simon maneuvered out of the neighborhood, grinning the whole way.

# CHAPTER 12

The car felt good. Cat-like was a decent description, it made almost no noise, but the noises it did make sounded, warm, welcoming, inviting, contented. Like it might jump up into your lap and start kneading your thighs. Except, that was ridiculous, obviously.

The rain started to increase, so Simon had to stop for a few moments at the first stop sign he pulled up to and calmly flip some switches, adjust some dials and feel genuinely confused, while he tried to figure out the windshield wipers.

*Shit, in this nice of a car, you'd think the wipers would be controlled by a goddam voice command.*

He finally found the right spot to turn them on. In his defense, he really didn't drive much. He had his license, sure, but when he was in the car it was usually with Logan, otherwise he typically biked all over town. He did prefer it usually, but on days like this, with the mounting rain and the puddles and sidewalk swamps accumulating more and more droplets, the car was definitely an improvement.

Simon felt cool, collected and confident. Despite having just committed grand theft auto, he wasn't as worried as one would think.

*I mean, Derek probably won't even put down his Xbox controller for another two hours, then he'll eat with his big idiot friends, then what? Get changed for a party? Or even just drink some expensive ass whiskey at home?*

This logic was enough for Simon at that moment, and otherwise, he just wanted to drive, live a little, feel like someone other than himself.

Swinging onto the highway and turning up the radio, he only had to go two exits north to get to Logan's house, but he wanted to warm that sucker up, really get it up to speed. Shoving his foot onto the gas pedal, he pushed down hard.

Since school had just got out, there wasn't rush hour traffic yet. The highway was pretty damn clear. He felt the car rumble steadily faster and faster. His adrenaline shot up as he got a bit nervous, this was where he was most likely to get caught. Going over the speed limit, he was now at a quick seventy miles per hour, and in a car that wasn't his. But he decided it just simply didn't matter.

Two exits later he merged easily back to the right and guided the car gently into Logan's neighborhood. Logan lived a little further from town proper, so from his house, they could take some windy back roads, hit the lake, sit at the park in the woods and just enjoy the quiet for a few minutes.

He swiveled into Logan's driveway, his cruddy little Honda sat out front, Logan was perched on the front porch smoking a joint. It appeared he had just arrived home because he hadn't even made it inside yet. Cell phone in hand, Logan looked up, pushing his eyebrows together in confusion. His mouth fell open when Simon jumped out of the driver side.

Simon flung his arms up into the air, as if to say "Ta-da!" and Logan's eyes got bigger, his mouth ajar, his joint slipping out of his right hand.

"What. The. Fuck. Simon" he stammered.

"Your chariot awaits, M 'Lord" Simon said in a pompous voice and gave a deep bow, chuckling, "and may I suggest, M'Lord than one shall not withhold thy weed. But is encouraged to pass on thy blunt to those weary from the daunting travels of the eve".

"What. The. Fuck. Dude!" Logan had put the burning bit of weed out and jumped up from his spot on the steps, his backpack still sitting in the chair next to the front door. Simon always liked Logan's house, it was large, immaculate, but homey, cozy and reasonable. With dark wood, an oversized porch, view of the lake and a tidy yard. The difference between Logan and Derek's houses was that Logan's felt full of love, like whoever took care of it, really cared and was proud of the home they created. Whereas, Derek's entire neighborhood felt like a big circle jerk of "mine is better than yours".

"I thought we could go for a drive"

"What are you doing? You fucking idiot. You're going to get arrested!" Logan finally let out a bit of a chuckle despite his shock.

"I'm not. I'll be fine, but that dickhead Derek deserves a bit of a scare. C'mon. . .let's take a drive. You got a lighter?" he responded confidently, gesturing at Logan's porch, where the lighter and smokables were left.

Logan gaped and reluctantly stepped backwards towards the house, snagged his backpack, tossed it in the house, his mom wasn't home yet. Grabbed a pack of cigarettes from a jacket pocket that was hanging just inside the door, a lighter and smiled nervously.

"You sure man? You know I'd love to piss my folks off right now but getting in serious trouble isn't the plan" he admitted, grimacing.

"It'll be fine. If anything, I'll take the fall. All is good. Get in. The seats are warm" he winked and slipped inside the car, as his friend propped the door open, sighed, smiled and crouched into the car.

The two boys sidled out of the neighborhood, they took the route at the back of the neighborhood, so they could immediately jump on the curvy road up the hill and around the lake.

It was one of those picturesque afternoons, yellow and orange foliage streaming past them in a blur, the leaves fluttering around the tires of the car, the light rain streaking across the windshield as the, now working, windshield wipers flicked the specks of water away every few seconds. Simon made sure to handle the car carefully and it responded with easy, smooth movements. The little coupe seemed to read his mind and he smiled the whole drive. Logan sat quietly in the passenger seat, grinning as well.

Both boys felt rebellious, free and happy in that moment. They both knew this was the wrong thing to do legally, but morally it didn't feel so bad.

Soon, Simon started to gently step on the brakes and flipped the right turn signal on and he eased the car down a small, gravel pathway, until they hit a practically empty parking lot. The only other car was a small white pickup that belonged to the park maintenance crew, so they knew they were safe and out of earshot of the law for a little while longer.

They took off on foot down a muddy, half gravel path through the damp leaves and prickly bushes. A few yards ahead was a clearing with plenty of light. When they got to the clearing, they had come to the edge of the stoic lake. The rain left little footprints briefly in the water as they landed softly. It smelled fresh, clean, and the slight pitter pattering of the rain was entrancing.

Logan pulled his hood up on his jacket and Simon smashed his beanie further down his forehead. They padded along the water edge and crept along the dock that jutted out over the water, to dangle their feet off the edge.

Neither of them had talked still, but they were both still smiling, despite being half soaked, at this point.

Logan lit up a cigarette, and handed another to Simon, who waited quietly for the lighter. They finally started talking.

"So, holy shit, this is insane" said Logan after taking a drag.

"Yeah, sorry man. I mean really, I don't want to get you in trouble. But it just felt *right*" Simon responded, give his friend an apologetic smile.

Logan started laughing, "You really are insane, but you know I'll be here for you. Thanks for including me in your bizarre need to teach the rich a lesson"

"Anytime, anytime." he sat quietly for a moment, "I know I go a little overboard sometimes. Or more than overboard," he chuckled, "but life just isn't fair sometimes. You know?"

He fell quiet, starred at his shoes, as he kicked his feet with the peaceful water glistening in the background. He frowned, the most serious he had been all day.

"I'm sorry" he finished.

"Don't be sorry. Don't even think about being sorry. You're right. Life isn't fair. It sucks, and good people get the short end of the stick. It's a massive bummer. And sometimes being a rebel vigilante is all you can do" Logan said, nudging Simon under the ribs with his elbow.

The boys looked at each other, Simon nodded slowly as he looked back at his feet, still nodding, face nondescript.

"At the risk of sounding obsessed with you or something; you're a great friend. Thanks, man" Simon chuckled.

"Anytime, you're my people, ya know?" Logan muttered back.

They finished their cigarettes in silence, a knowing mutual understanding of friendship, love and admiration for each other.

They lit up another, and finally started joking around

again, the seriousness wearing off, as they sunk into their usual form.

"So, Lyss fucking Rogers, huh?" snorted Logan.

"Yeah, man. She vill be mine" Simon responded in his Dracula voice. "But seriously man, more than meets the eye with that pretty gal. I'm going to get to know her. You mark my words. She should know that not all dudes are total pigs"

"Alright, alright, as long as she doesn't ever fuck with game nights, then I'm cool with it." Logan exclaimed as he tossed his hands in the air in defeat and understanding.

They kept talking animatedly for a while before Logan checked his watch.

"Hey, man. There is some stuff I gotta do tonight, Mom will be home soon. Mind if we take off?"

"Absolutely, I should get this damn car back anyway. I'm pretty sure I'll be in some shit soon" snickered Simon.

They made their way back through the small wooded area and to the car. Footprints sticking to the fresh mats in the car with the mud they drug in.

"I'll message you tomorrow" Logan said as he jumped out of the car when they arrived at his home. His mother's car perched in the driveway, and lights glimmering warmly inside.

Simon saluted him and instead of taking the car on the

highway, he took the back roads back to Derek's fancy ass neighborhood.

The closer he got to the house, the more nervous he became. Butterflies swarmed his stomach and he felt a little sick. As he made the last turn down the street Derek lived on, he started nervously laughing as he caught sight of red and blue lights smudging together as they spun wildly in the rain. It was starting to get dark out. He touched his left hand to his head and guffawed loudly.

He drifted slowly, but assuredly into the driveway. And without hesitation, slapped the car into park and got out of the car.

"You little shit! Do you know how much money my fucking car costs?" Derek, the hot head spits. God forbid he just calm down. Simon tried to stifle his smile.

"Evening son, my name is Officer Pedersen. It seems that, uh, you've brought this car you've stolen...back?".

If Simon didn't know better, he'd think that Mr. Pedersen was about to laugh as well.

Before Simon could respond a door slammed behind them, and a distinguished middle-aged man came strolling into the driveway. He directed his attention at the police officer.

"Mr. Pedersen, sir. There is no need to press charges

on this young man. I would, however, like his guardians to be aware, so they can punish him at their own discretion. It doesn't appear that there are any damages. Our friend here, seems to have taken a joy ride in my moronic son's car" he finished, hands on hips, glaring not at Simon, but at Derek. Who stared back, stunned and furious.

"Oh, okay, understood. It's your call. I'll still have to take him down to the station, get in touch with the folks. Get this all taken care of. We won't keep you any longer, if all looks good to you. Let me know if there is anything else I can do Mr. Stills. You know how to find me" Officer Pedersen said giving him a curt nod and looking in Simon's direction. He winks quickly at Simon, trying to hide another smile.

"DAD! What??? You're not going to PRESS CHARGES? Are you nuts?" shouted Derek.

"Son. Stop with that retched screaming, you sound like obscene, quite frankly. Number one, you need to learn a lesson about the safety of your personal property. This young man was able to *steal* your car without your detection for *hours*. Number two, most people don't commit crimes unless provoked. Now this fellow who stole your car is obviously going to get in trouble with his family" he finally looked at Simon carefully finally then continued, "but I have a very good bullshit detector, and son, you have certainly obtained some enemies. Go inside. No car for a week. And I don't want to hear another word"

Derek's face turned bright red, he looked like he may cry, and he spun around fast, almost lost his balance and stormed into the home.

"Do you mind if I speak with Simon quickly, Officer Pedersen?" Mr. Stills asked.

"Uh, sure if he's okay with it"

"Yeah...sure" Simon sputtered, holding Officer Pedersen's gaze, unsure of what may happen next.

Derek's father took his shoulder and guided him a few steps away.

"Now, I'm sorry for Derek. He's been quite the embarrassment lately. I hope that you do learn from this, it's not acceptable to steal and I'd hate to see someone from our lovely Hillvale end up on television one day for the crimes he's committed. But I assume you come from a loving family, so don't put them through hell. Be better than this ridiculous family that I've cultivated. Monsters. All of them" a note of disdain hung in the air, lingering around every word he muttered.

"Uh- yeah. O-okay sir. Thank you. I apologize for the inconvenience..." Simon trailed off, as Derek's father turned back to Officer Pedersen.

"Thank you again and have a good evening. Or the best you can, I imagine at least one of you will be getting quite a talking to tonight," he said glancing at Simon as he shook hands with the Officer, nodded and stalked toward the house.

"Alright, kiddo. Let's stick you in the back of the car. Want me to keep the lights on? They are kinda fun, we can go fast" Pedersen says in a mocking voice, nudging Simon playfully.

Simon looked at him and chuckled, still shocked at his luck.

"What Simon? You think I don't know these rich dicks are a bunch of assholes? Whatever, we'll let you off easy. I'll have to tell your folks something, but we'll keep it off your record. We all do stupid shit when we're young. I'm no exception. But don't think I'm not telling the whole family. The boys are gonna shit themselves when they find out you stole a damn car. You crazy bastard. You're lucky I was on patrol though!" he exclaimed, his eyes crinkling with a smile and looking slightly relieved. "And honestly, we were lucky that Mr. Stills wasn't more concerned. He may be a rich asshole, but he hates his family more than anything. Sad really".

Simon hopped in the back seat. "Thanks Chuck. And hey, I have classes with Tristan this quarter! Since Troy moved out, I haven't been around much, but I'll be in a homecoming group with your daughter next weekend, I think!" he said.

"That's great. I'm glad you two are still friends, even if her brothers are running around doing who knows what"

"All your kids are great. I'm thankful for the lot of ya. And, uhm, thanks again. I know I lucked out by having my childhood best friends' dad working tonight. But, I just got a little ahead of myself. I'm not a bad kid. I hope you know that" Simon muttered sheepishly.

"Oh, of course I know that. We just need to make sure your parents remember that when they ground you for the next 6 months. I was a bit like you as a kid. Hot headed, quick to action. It means you've got passion. And as long as that passion isn't for my daughter, then you're alright in my book. Plus, the whole damn family adores you" he said reassuringly and winked again.

"Oh!" Chuck practically shouted, "your bike is in my trunk, don't let me forget!"

The rest of the ride, they chatted about the family and school. Chuck had a certain calm about him, he made you feel like he was on your side. It made Simon forget a little bit about the significant problem he had just caused. He sighed with relief, contemplated what his evening had in store for him and hoped for the best.

# PART FOUR

*Seth*

# CHAPTER 13

Seth rolls over slowly in bed, dragging a bit of the thick, plush comforters with him. He squinted and squeezed his eyes, before cracking the corner of his right eye. Shifting slightly to face the rest of the dim bedroom. A small sliver of light beamed directly onto his forehead and into his face as he made small adjustments.

*Forgot to shut the blinds again, nice one Seth.*

Pots and pans clanged below in the kitchen directly under his bedroom. Seth's grandmother was, no doubt, making some intricate breakfast that she wouldn't touch, but would force Seth and his grandfather to swallow. She'd watch them with crinkles in the corners of her tired eyes, smiling with proud exuberance.

This was a normal morning occurrence, Grandma making food that she had no business dabbling in, then Seth and Grandpa would choke the food down in small gulps and plenty of water to wash it down. In her old age with her taste buds failing, she had decided to take up cooking, and the process was painful for everyone's gut. But Grandpa never said anything bad. He'd just sip coffee, peer over his newspaper and chide polite comments in her direction.

Seth often wondered if she knew they hated the food, or if she was completely oblivious. Or maybe it was her sly form of torture.

Using an arm to prop himself up to an elbow. He began grasping aimlessly for the thick black glasses perched on his nightstand amidst a pile of other items. His hand thumped around for a moment, coming in to contact with an empty bag of Cheetos and he managed to keep a plastic tumbler of Mountain Dew from toppling over before finally wrapping his fingers around the frames.

He fumbled and slapped the spectacles crookedly on his face, pushed his messy and greasy hair off his forehead. Reaching toward the foot of his bed, he yanked his laptop off the floor and into the bed. Quickly, he logged in to the backend of his website host site. Clicking rapidly, and navigating to the message box, scanning the messages about his latest posts. Smirking to himself and liking as many comments as he could through bleary, puffy morning eyes. He laughed aloud at some comments. The audience was dripping with sarcastic undertones. His favorite kind of humor. The kind of humor where you almost believe the comments are someone being truly unintelligent. Other messages on the posts posed questions about mediums, preferred software's and technique. The questions that required technical answers were always those that threw him off the most. Like people actually appreciated his style and wanted to know how to achieve the same thing. They wanted to utilize his knowledge and skill in their own work. It gave him an ounce of self-confidence. Some amount of authority. Others simply mentioned how "cool" or "fucking sweet, dude" the posts were.

He found that socializing with his followers and fans helped him to gain more views, not that views was the sole purpose of his work. It was about spreading and sharing. And there was something really exhilarating that happened online. It was simpler to find communities that appreciated you, easier to communicate when there were no pretenses of what you should be.

It should be noted that Seth was an artist. He used graphic design elements to create colorful pieces that were posted to his website, Imgur and Instagram accounts. The works were frequently stolen and shared around sites like Reddit, so he'd started adding watermarks. There had been requests in the past to sell prints, to do face reveals or

YouTube tutorials on his approach, but he couldn't bring himself to commit to those types of projects. Not yet, anyway.

Scrolling on still, he skimmed and read. Looked through other accounts and found motivation and interesting images that were unique, and he let them know he appreciated their efforts, too.

A soft knock on the door, interrupted his solace. Bringing him firmly back to reality. Time to get ready for school. High school and deal with the kids he didn't identify with.

"Honey buns, you up?" his grandmother chimed and cracked the door open, seeing the catastrophe inside for the first time in days. Since his room was upstairs, visitors didn't typically meander up the staircase, but Seth was running particularly late this morning, so his grandmother needed to poke at him a bit harder this morning.

She pushed the door open wide, while Seth sat distractedly in bed, clicking furiously through media, barely glancing up at her as fresh air finally punctured the dank air that was BO and sugary snacks. He tried to ignore her and seem busy, avoiding a confrontation with her was the best route in situations where she invaded his space.

"Seth! What is this mess? Now, you *know* we are flexible with you, but this is an *ABSOLUTE* mess! You are cleaning this tonight!" she said with finality, hands on hips and her brow furrowed, "And enough with this ridiculous internet thing every single morning. Don't you have any real friends to talk to? You shouldn't be spending all of your time staring at a computer screen!"

Her wrinkly hands flew up in exasperation, as she stared at him without getting a response. Setting the laptop down and closing it lightly, Seth looked back at her.

*Why is that somehow an issue? Don't people realize how much weight it holds to be involved in any kind of community?*

Seth pursed his lips lightly, not saying anything. Watching his grandmother's face turn to concern, he let it. She hurt his feelings and though she didn't mean to, she shouldn't feel good about the way she accused him. The guilt bubbled up and she sputtered at him.

"Sorry, hon. Just worry about you. Let's get this mess cleaned tonight, huh? Breakfast is soon" she trailed off lightly, with a soft apologetic smile. She twisted and wrung her hands, clearly uncomfortable. Losing her cool was uncommon, but spouting snide remarks wasn't.

Seth watched her go, backing out of the room slowly and shutting the door behind her with a soft click. Sighing heavily, he slipped out of bed.

His grandparents weren't always particularly sensitive.

The couple had been through a lot and their tough exterior bled over into their relationship with Seth, who they took in as a young tike.

They had adopted Seth just as he was starting second grade. His mother got too high one night. Crashed her car and died trying to get a quick fix down the road from their bug-ridden apartment. She was a young mother to start with and got involved in drugs early. It ended with meth. His father had been long gone, had slipped into the night, and eventually passed from an overdose before Seth was even born.

The family didn't discuss their daughter with Seth much. She had been a stunning, motivated teenager. One time at Thanksgiving Seth's aunt got a bit drunk and pulled Seth outside with her when she was smoking a secret cigarette. Her words fell out of her like a water fall.

"Your mother was stunning. But, there was so much pressure on her. And sometimes love makes you do dumb things. The drugs eased her anxiety for a while, I think. She was so excited about you, kid. Don't ever forget that. She loved you. But sometimes demons wake you up at night in the way a screaming child can't".

A moment later his grandmother flung the sliding door open, finding Seth hunched against the siding and his aunt with a crystal glass of wine tucked under one arm and the stub of cigarette up to her mouth. His aunt had rolled her eyes at the glower she was met with, flicked the butt into the grass.

"I just wanted you to know that, Seth. You deserve better than..." she whispered to him before stepping inside.

"Stop" his grandmother hollered, looking hysterical, "Stop. It's a happy night. Now get inside".

That was the last time anyone in his family mentioned his parents.

Considering the circumstances, Seth was relatively well adjusted. He wasn't particularly social. And maybe that wasn't his fault. The silence that surrounded his flesh and blood was stunted, and he didn't have many people he related to. The Hillville area didn't respect drug addicts and there was tendency to look down on their spawn, too. Seth found he was met with a lot of derision and his peers weren't interested in his preferred topics, anyway. Ivy-league colleges and designer clothes didn't matter to him much.

Seth did appreciated everything his grandparents had done for him. Their daughter had been nothing but challenging, they appreciated that Seth was smart and *clean*. Clean in an addiction sense, anyway. Though, Seth sensed that they thought technology was an addiction. His grandfather held this bizarre, and rather old school opinion that the internet was dangerous and could take over lives. More than a little dramatic, but maybe they had reason to be paranoid.

But they were supportive, at least. Buying him technology, supporting his skills and interests, they approved of his school work efforts and were happy to help him. While they weren't always understanding, they were certainly happy to spend their fortune on him staying busy. They'd pay for colleges, too. He was fortunate in that sense. But his grandparents were the types who thought jobs could only be simple titles; doctor, lawyer, salesman.

As Seth got older and had more freedom, he found his own communities online, and his grandparents simply didn't understand it. They didn't realize that friends could be faceless people you have never met in person. Because of this, he kept to himself. Limited his verbal communication and worked on his graphic design. If he was being honest with himself, art was the goal.

Proceeding with the morning requirements, Seth stumbled around the large bedroom, flinging bits of clothing items into his arms and over his shoulder. Attempting to discern one shirt from another. At first glance the shirts were identical. Black, worn with printed graphics. Piles of flannels and different colored hoodies hung over the edge of the bed frame, making it near impossible to tell which items were clean and which were due for a wash.

Seth turned on some music, hopping around the different piles throughout the bedroom. Sound was never an issue at home. He could crank music up, watch movies at the highest volume and shout expletives while gaming without worrying about bothering anyone. Reason being that Seth had the entire second floor of the home to himself.

His grandparents stayed on the first level of the home, mainly because the master bedroom was on the first floor, which had been good planning when they shopped for their retirement home. His hardened grandfather spent most of his days in his study and his grandma flitted about the house, fussing over cleaning, the garden and ran copious amounts of errands with her "gal pals".

So, Seth could go days without running in to them. Summer break and weekends reflected this well. He'd hide out upstairs, blasting music and turning the volume of his video games, laughing loudly over his streaming mics. Only occasionally would he run into his grandma while he snuck fizzy drinking and salty snacks out of the pantry after dinner. The alone time was ideal.

Seth, now loaded his arms completely with clothing,

flicks the door open tactfully with his foot and totters down the hall. Walls covered with photos of trips, school photos, none of which feature his mother or father. Not even glancing at the walls, he pushes the bathroom door open by pushing his back in to it and tosses all the clothes into his laundry hamper, ditching his current clothes too and hops into the shower.

As he finishes getting ready for the day, he kicks a few items into his closet and under the bed.

*Less work later.*

Finally, school ready, with a packed book bag, the shiny laptop tucked delicately inside, along with headphones. Seth stumbled out of his room, supplies dangling off one arm, and the other dragging the bundle of laundry behind. The basket thumped loudly on each step slowly, careful not to let it totter over and splay clothes down the staircase.

Breakfast is quick and relatively painless. A pile of runny scrambled eggs was piled onto a plate while propped up at the breakfast bar in the large kitchen. The old man grips a coffee mug in the adjoining seat, eyes sliding quickly across the morning's newspaper. Chattering and clanging continues in the kitchen, as his grandmother tosses dishes into the dishwasher without rinsing, tops off the water in a flower vase and wipes down the counter before snatching the half-finished eggs out from under Seth's nose.

"So, I'll drop Seth off at school, head to the club to get in some Pilates, then I have some items to exchange at the boutique with Marie and we'll probably get lunch. Then I'll get Seth from school" she went into details about her plans for the remainder of the weekend. Seth and his grandfather nodded politely whenever she glanced up to smile at them. Neither cared nor paid much attention when she began her long ramblings.

"Oh, goodness, the time!" his grandmother exclaimed after a moment of silence where she was able to check the time, "We should get going Seth. Have everything?" she exclaimed without waiting for an answer. Ushering Seth out the door and into the car.

The car ride was full of more chattering, Seth nodded, half smiled and shrugged at all the appropriate moments.

When they arrived, she put the car all the way into park at the corner of the school and turned in her seat to look at Seth.

"Seth-y, I'm worried about you. You seem...more distant that normal. Are things okay? I know we are hard on you, and life hasn't been the easiest, but we do love you, dear" she smiled a sad but sincere smile. Her eyes seemed to glisten a bit, which made Seth feel guilty. He didn't feel okay.

But she was too wonderful to need worry about him in her life.

He finally spoke after a few calculating moments, trying to decide how to respond.

"Love you. I'm good" and stared her in the eye, expressionless and without smile.

"Okay, I love you, too," she nodded looking at her lap, "Well, have a nice day, I'll pick you up at 2:30".

He reached for the car handle and disappeared into the crowd of students, she watched him go for a moment, wondering if he was telling her the truth, decided to accept his answer and went on her way. That was always her weakness, accepting lies at face value.

# CHAPTER 14

I nstinctively slipping headphones into his ear, Seth nonchalantly drifted into school. The headphones allowed for the ignorance of surroundings, the defiance of any potential conversations and the ability to focus on one's own thoughts. Seth had mastered the ability to be invisible in the hallways. He would have been a perfect target for bullying if he were more accessible, but he kept his head down, his thoughts to himself and stayed far away from the assholes that stalked for victims.

At the insistence of his grandmother, Seth had tried to be social a few times. At one point, joining the Tech Club seemed like a good idea. But, much to his disappointment, the club focused heavily on gossiping about games and apps, as opposed to creating anything. He ditched the club as quickly as he had joined it.

Later, he became a regular fixture at the local card and game store, where weekly Dungeons and Dragons campaigns were held. The crew was funny and vague friendships were formed for a while.

The first few weeks of gaming with the D&D group was enjoyable. There were these glimmers of kinship amongst the group and being surrounded with people who had similar interests was oddly refreshing. They thrived on nerd culture. Discussions about comics and movie adaptations weren't uncommon. Seth's confidence boosted during his stint at the card shop, finding this group of people showed him that he wasn't an oddball, other people shared his passions. But soon, the game but soon, the quests failed to hold his interest. The card shop got cliquey and school interfered with his ability to make it in regularly. Even though he wasn't a regular fixture at the table anymore, Seth did finally decide to start sharing his art online with the encouragement of a few fellows he met during the D&D tournaments.

Much to his astonishment, he slowly developed a following online. He had created an Instagram account to start. It was easy to make, he didn't need to share any details about himself and people really liked his work. Then came the website and the Imgur account, so others could share his work on Reddit and other platforms with ease.

People liked his art, they liked his voice, which boarded on severe sarcasm. But he was relatable. He detailed epic stories and scenes and sometimes things as simple as classrooms and daily life. Posting anonymously allowed him to be himself. No pretending, no expectations and no embarrassment.

The community that presented itself, welcomed him with open arms. Doling out advice, learning and improving was inevitable. After all of his success online, he hoped that post-high school life would allow him to go to an art school. Continuing to build a career out of art, design and writing quickly became the dream.

Portfolio submissions were coming close and that scared Seth. If he applied to the few schools he was interested in, he'd need to finally slap his name on his work. His real name. No more hiding behind a brightened screen and the keyboard. He'd need to show the admission boards his work, who he was and what he was capable of, and his online platform was his best portfolio. An active, working online community. What could prove his worth better than that? That was terrifying though.

Giving up anonymity meant giving up his front. It also meant he'd need to discuss his work and prospects with his grandparents. After all, they'd be supplying the admission checks and *keen* didn't describe his grandfather's thoughts on art.

These are things that Seth thought about regularly and pondered that morning on his stroll to class. *Can my online persona meld together with my real life? Can my family get behind this? If I tell them, they'll see my graphic dick drawings, ughhhhhh.*

At this moment; he became aware of Homecoming approaching. Everyone around seemed to buzz, like they had all bathed in a vat of coffee and snorted a lot of coke. Everyone twitched with excitement, chatted endlessly and bounced in their seats.

Sometimes Seth felt like he was standing still, while everyone moved in hyper speed around him. Like the opening scene of *Limitless* where things fly by quickly and you feel like you're getting vertigo.

The first half of the day consisted of jotting down notes, copying quotes of those around him into speech bubbles. Drawing illustrations of classmates and creating new word letterings. Every few minutes, a worthy comment would be made by an instructor and made it to the main notes part of the notebook paper. He was a good student and was able to glean the most necessary info from simply looking through material and staying relatively caught up on assignments.

Despite his success online and with his work, Seth often felt bad. He was overweight, played video games, wasn't affiliated with anyone from school and felt disconnected from his reality. Even if he was interacting in real life, he wasn't dealing with *real* topics or materials. Most of his time was spent holed up in his room, playing video games on Xbox Live, drawing and researching schools.

Technically he was depressed, though not medicated. The word "lazy" had tumbled out of his grandfather's mouth on numerous occasions. Years of overprotection and avoidance of anything "scary" took a toll on his ability to be personable. But aren't all creatives a little nutty?

*I'm not lazy, just lazy at traditional things. Is it so bad to be motivated by different outcomes?*

Trekking through the day, indifferently. Wrinkling his forehead and pushing his glasses high up on the bridge of his nose regularly which slipped frequently because his head was constantly pointed straight down at his paper, where he sketched.

Today, he started on a piece that was larger, and emotional. Emotional wasn't his brand.

But it seemed fitting. The thoughts were on the forefront of the mind and the piece was intuitive. Scribbling quick notes on the edges of the paper about coloring and little quotes that could be incorporated into the illustration, then shaded and worked furiously, until suddenly the bell chimed for lunch.

Leaving class, he pushed against the crowds skipping in the opposite direction. He was the salmon in the river of students. Stepping through the threshold of the library, a sigh of relief left him.

The library, an oasis. A place to be alone for a solid thirty minutes. Access to art materials, to computers and scanners and the best Wi-Fi in the school.

Upon entering, he waved hello to the middle-aged librarian Mrs. Picks.

"Good Afternoon Seth! How are you today?" she smiled widely.

"Uh- I'm good. How are you, Mrs. Picks?" he muttered back.

"Oh good. You know me. Mainly picking up after uncourteous students" she rolled her light eyes, "What are we working on today? Shall I boot up the scanner?"

"That'd be great actually. I am going to colorize this image today but need to scan the original first" he finished flatly.

Mrs. Picks gestured at the seat next to her desk with a smile and spun around in her chair to turn on the scanner behind her. It was a fancy, high quality scanner and printer, but the machine was a bit loud and got really warm, so Mrs. Picks didn't keep it on all day. It got the most use when Seth needed to scan another image.

He plopped down in the chair and extracted his laptop and a bag of gummy worms from his bag, opening them wide, and pushed it between himself and Mrs. Picks. Who idly stuck her thin hand into the bag, picking out a small handful of the squishy candy, while Seth stepped behind the counter and began to set up his image.

"Are you going to show me your illustrations today, Seth? Or is this one not even close?" she asked.

"Not sure," he responded distractedly. He had his finger to his lips, assessing his options at the scanner. "I think I want to get this one completely done before I post or show. I don't think I want early criticism".

"No problem! Plans this weekend, then?" she said, while taping away at her computer, answering emails and munching away at Seth's snack.

"Nope. Of course not"

Mrs. Picks was Seth's favorite person at school and she wasn't even one of his peers. He spent most of his lunch times in the library, sucking on sweets and chatting with her while he worked on personal projects. The supportive librarian was his biggest fan and the only person who knew about Seth's secret life online as an art content creator. She followed and liked every single one of his posts, while this was typically frowned upon, they had justified their friendship outside of school because she wasn't *supposed* to know it was him and said she would simply deny knowledge if ever asked. They had laughed at that.

Mrs. Picks was pregnant with her first child. Seth had been excited for her but was sad to learn she'd be on maternity leave later that year. When he found out, he began to bring sweets every day for them to share.

"What are you doing Seth? Trying to plump me up even more?" she had laughed as she devoured a handful of peanut M&M's one afternoon.

The remainder of the lunch was spent in relative silence, as the pair slurped up gummy worms. Seth was beginning to color his image in Photoshop, and Mrs. Picks texting her husband a nice message and opening a new shipment of textbooks.

The top of the hour rang clear, the buzzer signaling the end of lunch sounded. Seth clicked save multiple times over, plagued with paranoia after many saving disasters. His vibrantly colored image glared back at him. He blinked rapidly and rubbed his eyes under his glasses. Sometimes working on the computer left him feeling as though he hadn't blinked in ages.

He cocked his head sideways like a dog, zoomed out of

the image to get a bigger impression of the piece as a whole. Staring. His stomach sunk but his heart warmed. It was finally a piece that made him feel something a little more *real*. It wasn't a joke. It wasn't drenched with scorn. The colors wrapped and twisted with vibrancy amongst a dark and dreadful scene.

One more click of the save button and he slapped the computer shut.

"Have a nice weekend, Seth! Can't wait to see the final product!" Mrs. Picks said with an encouraging and honest smile.

"You have a good weekend too. Tell your husband I told him to give you a foot massage" he said back.

"PFFT! Yeah right! We'll probably devour some pizza and I'll stare longingly at the wine cabinet" she said, touching her bulbous belly.

"Have fun. See you Monday" he said with a wave and sauntered into the hallway once again.

Leaving lunch in the library was the worst part of the day because Mrs. Picks was the highlight.

The school day ended anti-climactically. He stored his books in his locker and headed to the parking lot and gazed over the line of cars, until he spotted the forest green Mercedes and bumbled over and got into the car with his grandmother. And the rest of the way home was filled with words, but none of them his.

# CHAPTER 15

The remainder of the blustery afternoon is spent driving around to various stores with Seth's grandmother. For a woman who is always busy, running errands and shopping during the day, it was always shocking how many more stops they needed to make on the way home.

They pop by the public library to return a tattered romance novel then to the grocery store. An unnecessary adventure, Seth knows because they'll end up ordering pizza.

"What do you want me to get you?" Grandma says before flinging the door open and dashing into the store.

"The usual. Chips and sodas. That's fine" Seth responds, stepping out and speed walking to get under the awning. Typically, when his grandmother makes a grocery run, he'll head to game store.

Brushing rain off his head as he steps into the familiar space. The store was littered with different board games, video game consoles and comic books.

The store is small but well laid out. In the far back is a small area with pinball and soda machines, so some kids are hanging out in the back, slapping the sides of the dinging machine. The sales associate is leaning on the counter and gives Seth a head nod as he comes in.

"Hey man. Let me know if you need anything" he drones and continues to flick through a pile of second hand games.

"Thanks, just killing time today" Seth mumbles and stalks through the store.

He stalks around the store, hands in pockets, taking in the new games that are on display and mentally noting to look up the reviews before deciding if he'll buy any. Losing himself in some comic books, he flicks through, acknowledging the small, defined lines and distinct moment when dialogue is needed. Comics were an interesting medium to Seth, and graphic novels even more so.

A few moments later, as he's studying the works in a new super hero book, his phone vibrates in his pocket, a text from his grandma letting him know she's back at the car.

On his way out, he buys two new comics, the cashier double bags them in the slim paper sheets that they usually use to help keep the rain from penetrating. They nod at each other once more before he heads out the door, keeping his head low as he gets in the car.

When they arrive at home, Seth runs up the stairs catching his breath at the top and flings his backpack onto his large squishy bed. Pulls out his head phones and laptop and dips into his beanbag chair that's propped in front of his large television and gaming area.

Seth had been allowed to design his own bedroom when he was 15 and luckily, he hadn't changed too much since then, so the space worked well.

The bedroom is large, it was more of a bonus room than a bedroom. In one corner of the room, he has three large beanbag chairs ("for your friends" his grandma had said) and they all faced a very large, mounted television screen. Lining the wall, a sleek entertainment system framed the television and housed all of his game consoles. An Xbox, PlayStation and Wii. The shelves were heavy with game cases for each console and a collection of favorite films. Many nights had been spent plopped down in the beanbag chair, snacking, playing and getting lost in game play.

Before beginning a new game, he flicks open the illustration. Adding details and refining.

The piece makes him feel empty and sad. The illustration puts his vacant and distant thoughts into the universe. It accurately acknowledges the passion and need to create. Almost two hours go by while focusing on wrapping up the work.

A quick *bbbbring* comes from downstairs and interrupts his stream of thoughts and extracts him from the work.

*Doorbell. . . must mean pizza. Grandma will holler at me in a minute.*

Taking the moment of clarity, he takes a critical look at the picture. A weight seems to have lifted from his chest. A smile stretches wide, as he admires the work.

Confidence seeps into him. Pushing himself out of the beanbag, preparing to head downstairs for dinner.

*This is it. This is the moment to talk to them about this work I've been doing. . .*

He pads down the stairs and into the kitchen. Palms sweating but knowing it's now or never.

There are a few blackened dishes piled in the sink and the odor of burned food lingers slightly in the air. Seth pulls up a chair across from his grandfather and grandma emerges from the kitchen with a pile of napkins and a few paper plates.

"Hope everyone is hungry! I ordered pizza. . .the uh, the oven was acting funny, so my initial plans for dinner fell through. Sorry about the wait" she stammered as she sat down and served herself a slice.

DOWN THE PRIMROSE PATH

Only a grunt of approval parts his grandfather's lips. Seth nodded and proceeded to coat his slice in parmesan and pepper flakes.

"So, young man. How was school?" his grandfather murmurs after a few minutes, "Got any big plans this weekend?" He raises an eyebrow underneath his thin glasses and glances at Seth disapprovingly, knowing full well that no plans had been made.

"Uh- school's fine" Seth mumbled, glancing up and catching his eye before taking a bite.

Before his grandfather could question him further, Grandma launched into her story about her afternoon with Marie and their old lady escapades.

Seth ate quietly, thinking of how best to bring up his hopes for college, how best to explain his online success. While his grandfather grunted at his wife's stories and nodded calmly. Seth's heart raced.

*Will they understand my work? They can't be that surprised right? They think I'm just fucking around playing video games, they will definitely be happy that I'm at least doing something healthy and productive. They have to. Art is art. Who doesn't like art?*

"And then Marie says to m-"

"I have something to say" Seth says, cutting his grandma off. Wiping his mouth gingerly, looking at this plate, tucking both arms under the table.

"Oh, the boy speaks" his grandfather rolls his eyes, "maybe a new computer this time? Another Game Box? Must be something important if he is going to interrupt someone mid-story".

"Y-yes, sir," Simon stutters, shocked that his grandfather has already made this difficult and he'd only said a few words. He cleared his throat. "I'd like to talk to you about something important, something that I've been, uh-, doing and working on".

His grandmother's eyes got big and she set her napkin down.

"What is it Seth-y? You're scaring me" she mutters, reaching for her husband's hand in support.

"No, it's-it's not like that Grandma. So, you know how I'm always in my room? You think I'm always just gaming or playing games, or-or whatever. But I'm not always doing that," he says delicately, trying to maintain his calm and confidence under the glare of his grandfather.

His grandmother's lip trembles, no doubt terrified that not only is her grandson finally talking in full sentences to her again, but probably afraid he'll admit that he's on the same drugs that killed his mom.

"I've been doing a lot of drawing" he blurts and looks

at them both in the eye.

His grandmother lets out a sigh of relief, "Oh, that's nice honey" and moves to take a bite of her crust.

"Drawing, huh? Sounds like an interesting *hobby*." his grandfather responds, derision engulfing the last word. He eyes his grandson closely, knowing the conversation isn't over.

"Yeah, it's more than a hobby though, I guess. I've been posting my work online. Sharing it with some online communities. It's getting a lot of attention. Um-lots of people like my work, and my writing too, actually. And I was hoping to show you and maybe talk about my plans for my working on it and school...." he trailed off, seeing the laughter in his grandpa's eyes.

"Ha! Plans, huh? What you think you're going to be the next Van Gogh? Do some doodles for children's books? What sort of plans can there possibly be for a *hobby*? And drawing is nothing but a hobby" his grandfather sneered at him, clearly disappointed and annoyed at the conversation. The only conversation they'd had in months.

"Go on, honey" his grandmother urged, her brows furrowed again and looking at her husband says, "Let him finish, my god."

"I, uh, think I'd like to make this a career. I'd like to go to college for this. For art. Get some more training, get some job or internship opportunities and make designing a, like a thing for me" he said quickly, sure to avert eye contact after getting it out.

"No," said his grandfather. "I'm not going to let all the time and money we've spent on you go to waste for some silly pipe dream in *art*. It's not feasible and I'm not letting anyone else in my family become a-, become a loser again" he managed to get out. He also avoided eye contact with Seth at this point but was steadfast in his anger.

"Russell!" exclaimed his grandmother, "Why would you say such a thing? Just because we have had issues in our family, does not mean that Seth is a *loser*. He is just working for something" she turned to Seth, "I'd love to see your work, honey".

Seth was already gone.

He harbored high hopes this would be a productive conversation. Instead, the talk was halted without so much as a discussion or a few moments' thought. Seth hardly spoke to the family, finally he opened up and got shot down immediately.

His grandfather was a straightforward man, he had little respect for anyone unless they made money and "pulled their weight in society". He hoped and expected Seth to make his way into a reasonable, steady work force. Russell wanted success for his grandson, the same success he wanted for his crack head daughter.

Seth plopped down in the bean bag again and delved into the false world within a first-person shooter game.

Light knocking danced on the door which was ignored.

After a few rounds in the game, his watch read 8:15pm. The night was young, and it was prime time for posting on Instagram. Remaining on the menu, he fished his laptop off the ground and exported his newest illustration.

He wrote the caption: "Frustration clouds me" and posts.

The image is intricate, vibrant and terrifying, compared to other illustrations, which usually consist of characters doing funny things or fighting a villain and a string of clever captions. But this felt more dramatic and revealing. Not to mention the focus was on a character who resembled Seth, giving away his age and his fears.

Bold colors, the theme was a smattering of blues, oranges and reds, making it seem epically interesting but dense. It depicted a teenager in a crib, with his head tucked between his knees, as if crying, as a cloud of smoke wafted through the air overhead. The boy depicted is wearing something like Seth's typical choice of outfit, a black shirt and red flannel left open, his pudgy stomach visible. Then a sea of people, heads were distorted and covered by the billowing fumes, to save their identity from being revealed. They had speech bubbles poking out, an idea he borrowed from the classic comic book style, hauntingly with things that said, "loser", "friendless", "who are you?" etc. The illustration made Seth feel proud, feel vulnerable, strong and scared.

That's it. Simply that. He was able to voice his primary issues in the short caption. It's funny how writing things down makes problems seem much smaller than we regard them internally.

He was still angry, nervous and confused about how to convince his grandpa to get on board with the writing, drawing and content he created.

The community online didn't frighten him. They may call him a pussy or make fun of this new style of work, but it was manageable. Delete-able.

Back to fantasy. He sunk back into the comfort of gaming for a few more hours.

# CHAPTER 16

Eyes burned, and stomach growled. The clock read 10:26pm. A few hours of gaming can fly by quickly and he wasn't ready to be done. But, a break was necessary.

*I need some caffeine.*

Groaning while making use of his legs again, he glanced at his computer and swept it up, cracked it open and started getting nervous to check his account.

*Moment of truth. Refresh, I guess.*

The page loaded. There were 3,658 likes on the image. After only a few hours and plenty of comments as well. No hashtags, no specific attention drawn to it. Seth sat down, intrigued.

Wading through the comments he found some were other artists, commenting on line work, color choices and so on, simply being critical, like normal. Other people made comments about how this piece spoke to them, how they appreciated this, and were excited to see personal stuff from him. A few comments were shitty, but that was to be expected. The post was successful, a genuine surprise.

After a few moments of taking in the success of the post; he ventured into his direct messages, scrolling quickly, only a few messages. Some were left over from a few days prior with some fans or other artists. He knew he needed to respond, but that was for another day. Then one name stuck out. Stuck out like a sore thumb.

Logan Wheeler.

From school. His school at Hillvale. They had gone to school together forever, he was best friends with Simon, a funny kid with a bad attitude. They even had AP English together and regularly partnered for peer editing. Seth always thought Simon and Logan seemed like good guys, but why was Logan messaging.

*He isn't a fan, right? He couldn't know who I am?*

He opened the message:

"Hey man. I'm a big fan of your work. I don't know how many people send you these messages, so maybe this will get lost among your comments and messages, but I figured I'd say something anyway. . . I have my fair share of problems, trust me. And my best friend is a bit of a mess right now too. I just want you to know that there are so many people out there who look up to you, enjoy your work and want to see you continue. So, whatever's going on in your life, I hope that it doesn't keep you from living your best life. Sorry if this is kind of cheesy, but I'd want to hear it if I felt a little lost. That's what friends are for, and this online community is full of your friends. 'Night man. Good luck".

Seth's eyes welled with tears.

Shocked and completely put off by having a message from a classmate and a fan of his work. A friend. Maybe the pretentious school he attended did have some people worth befriending.

Logan was right though, in his message, the people who supported him online were his friends. They supported and followed and kept up to date on all of his work. The support he needed existed, and it proved his success.

Seth wrote back, "You have no idea how much that message helped." and shut his computer before he could think twice.

Standing up and pacing around the room for a few minutes, feeling strong and exhilarated again. Picking up his laptop, taking a deep breath then flinging the door open and stomping down stairs, where he could hear his grandparents chatting quietly as the television puttered along.

They were going to listen this time, hear what he had to say They were going to take these possibilities seriously.

He wanted to go to school for this. To make art his life. Proving this was something that *could* be profitable. It *would* be fulfilling. This was the first step toward making his real life, a little less sluggish.

# PART FIVE

*Logan*

# CHAPTER 17

The morning was drab. And the sky, beginning to lighten, crept through the mid-length curtains in Logan's disheveled bedroom. He sat upright in bed before his alarm was able to complete its morning task. Headphones donned and laptop, you guessed it, in his lap.

He jumped as the phone on his night stand spat indie music suddenly, signaling the school day was to begin soon. Putting his bronze hands up over his face, cold from lack of circulation, he massaged his eye balls.

Willing them out of their defunct, crispy, dried out state. The blinking and rolling around of eyes allowed them to move freely, coating them with moisture. Dragging himself out of the steady-eyed, stare he had been in.

Sweeping long legs up into his hands and tugging gently at the cushy woolen socks that had become twisted around and scooted out of bed. He perched on the edge and gingerly picked up the airplane shooters from the same table his phone rested on. Raised his hands over his head, creating a ninety-degree angle with his forearms and shot each miniscule plastic bottle across the room towards the trash can he had in the corner.

"Kobe!" he mumbled as the bottles bumped into the wall before falling onto the floor, missing the bin entirely. He smirked, and started tugging off his clothing, scratching his head as he made his way to the bathroom.

After it ran for a few moments he stepped lightly into the hot water. Smearing scented products and soap all over, trying to push the deliriousness of exhaustion away. Before leaving, he flung the shower handle to the right, switching the water to a freezing cold temperature immediately.

"Ah!"

Goose bumps emerged on his skin, but he did feel more awake. He only did this when he was hungover. It reminded him of those old western films when the sheriff was passed out drunk and a hero character came along and dunked the drunken fools face into a barrel of cold water, in attempts to sober him. The old trick worked surprisingly well for Logan. Sleep nearly erased, he hopped out of the cold water before he caught hypothermia. Coffee would take care of the rest.

Wrapping the towel around his slender body, he reached into the medicine cabinet and extracted the familiar white bottle of what his younger self called, "head ache pills".

Tossing the ibuprofen into the back of his throat and sipping water out of the facet, he thought back to the regretful concoction of soda and rum he had mixed the night before.

Before dressing, he had limited success flattening his wet hair in the mirror. But no problems arose when he ran through the list of assignments he completed the previous evening. Despite the "don't-give-a-fuck" attitude he exuded around his mother and friends, he definitely wanted to make the most of his schooling. Almost all subjects came easily to him and getting into a good school would be his ticket out of town next year.

Hillvale was a boring, mostly uppity community full of adults who had once been young professionals that settled in Hillvale to pump out some kids. There was a quaint downtown area, plenty of coffee shops and a well-rated high school that everyone in the area went to.

Hillvale was about 45 minutes from the next big town, and Logan wanted to get *at least* that far after graduation. Being on his own and starting to work towards his own future, was important to him.

He tottered around his bedroom, picking up school

books, plugging his laptop into the charger and tucking a recently rolled spliff into his desk drawer.

Tugging his favorite hoodie over his baggy button up and adjusting his jeans over his brand new Vans, he glanced in the mirror briefly, seeing traces of his father in his eyes. Then made his way downstairs for some food and hopefully very little conversation with his mother.

In the hall, he could hear his mom, still in her bathroom, hot tools clattering, a pffffssstttt sound from hair spray and she was obviously talking to someone on speaker phone.

"Mrs. Rogers please! Yes, I can hold...that's fine" she sighed heavily, her voice lined with tired disappointment.

Logan shook his head and galloped down the stairs. A pile of mail was flung on to the "Oh, Hello" door mat. Flicking his head back in the direction of his mother's bedroom up the stairs before picking it up, he bent down to snag the small stack of snail mail.

This was one of the more charming things of the Ethers' neighborhood, the homes had mail flaps in the doors still, so Karen, Logan's mom, had a nice relationship with their mailman, Chip. And gave him Starbucks gift cards during the holidays. This explained why mail was always crowding the front door.

*Too bad we probably won't live here much longer* Logan thought bitterly.

Scanning the envelopes, he began to rip everything to pieces. Bills, what appeared to be a wedding invitation, a card from Karen's work. Everything was destroyed, except for the Valpak. Keeping at least one piece of garbage mail helped him to avoid suspicion from his mom.

Logan had a very specific level of bitterness towards his mother. His folks had recently announced they were getting divorced, separated, whatever. Adults always had different words for what was basically the same thing. They weren't going to stay together and that broke up Logan's family. Simple as that.

And his father had left. Quickly, too. He packed and took off before the end of the school year the previous year and hadn't returned since. He'd already moved to a city on the other side of the state, found some hot younger woman and begun the process of settling back down. Logan dreaded to think about having a new sibling, but the possibility was inevitable.

"Your mother just isn't who she used to be. Bitch of a woman, that one. I'm sorry, kid" he had said in his manly, gravelly voice, as he clapped his son on the back, "I just can't live with this anymore, you must understand. It's nothing to do with you, son" he continued sadly, embracing him, enveloping him fully in his thick, dark arms.

"You'll be back, right? Holidays? Weekends? We can see each other. . ." Logan stammered, as tears started to bubble up in the corner of his eyes, still stunned. Hoping that this wasn't the truth.

"Of course, of course. You're my number one, Log. I'll call soon, and we can make plans. This is the best for everyone" he said confidently as he lowered himself into his perfectly manicured luxury car.

"'Kay" Logan said, crossing his arms over his chest and training his eyes on the pavement.

His father rolled down his window as he flipped the car into reverse, "Logan, I love you. Don't forget it", a big smile stretching across his animated face.

Logan gave him a light smile, nodded, "Love you".

Then his father backed out, blasted some music, as if it were victory music. Laughed out loud and tore out of the neighborhood. Leaving his son pressing his thumbs into his eyes, trying to stop the tears. He had fumbled his way back into the house, where his mother sat with a cup of tea in front of her. Her head draped delicately into her manicured hands.

In that moment, Logan couldn't have hated her more.

Her perfection, her need to nag, her smiley demeanor on a regular basis.

Her shoulders had been shaking slightly, as small tear drops slipped through the cracks of her fingers and her tea began to cool with peppering's of salty tears.

"He'd be staying if you'd been easier to deal with" Logan sneered at her, hot tears pouring from his face.

She had looked up, shocked, scared. Her eyes blood shot, her hands now covering her mouth. She just looked back before saying, "You don't know the half of it, Logan" softly.

"Doesn't matter now, he's gone" and he sprinted up the stairs and collapsed on his bed while Simon called him repeatedly.

That was 5 months ago. His dad had called every other week since, but never made plans. Logan texted him updates and received thumbs up emoji's in response to good news and very little else. The last time he had called there was a giggle and squeaky voice in the back ground. No doubt his dad's new woman. The one who got to keep him even though she didn't deserve it. Logan had come to convince himself that his mother was the villain in the story. Andre had been his hero growing up and his father being at fault wasn't something Logan was prepared to admit.

Since then, Logan hadn't apologized to his mom. They never talked about it. Instead his mother worked, made phone calls, and slapped a half-assed attempt at a smile on her face. But Logan could hear her crying at night. Sometimes his heart panged with guilt, but he couldn't bring himself to forgive her, for driving his flesh and blood away.

So, instead of letting himself feel bad, he held on to his grudges. He used his anger to cause small and wrathful inconveniences for his mother. Like throwing away bills and mail and leaving the kitchen window open in the rain. These small acts made him feel better in some twisted way.

Logan riffled through the immense kitchen pantry and pulled out some pop tarts wrapped in the silvery crinkle paper and poured a glass orange juice. He sat quietly, looking outside as the impending rain filled sky. Listening to his mother tromp down the stairs in her heels.

"G' Morning, Logan. How did you sleep?" she smiled knowingly at him, as she pulled some yogurt from the stainless-steel fridge. Her smile was genuine this morning though, the little creases in the corner of her eyes made an appearance.

"Fine" he mumbled back at her, not returning her playful salutation.

She put her hands on her hips and jokingly said, "Well

Mr. Talkative, how about a night in with Mom tonight? I was going to get a bunch of movies and binge. I'll even share some wine with you if you stay in".

Their family always drank with the kids. Even Logan's grandparents let him drink with dinner if he wanted, so alcohol wasn't something unusual in his household. Andre always joked that it was the most European thing about their family, despite their low percentage of European descent. That morning it was Karen's attempt at being a fun mom, a mom who couldn't get through to her kid. A mom who needed something, anything to be in touch with him.

"Nah. I got stuff with Si" he said without looking up from his crumbling mess of a pastry.

"Oh, okay!" she said, clearly disappointed, "What are you two getting up to?"

"I don't know. We haven't made plans yet"

She dropped her spoon, stared at it, and sighed, "Right. Okay. Well, let me know where you are, okay?" she was back to mom mode. Her disappointment rang clear, which made Logan feel a little bit better, even though guilt plagued his heart. Bittersweet.

"I'm out" he said as he swept up his bag, leaving his crumbs dispersed on the counter along with the shiny silver wrapper.

"Logan. . .aren't you going to. . . never mind" she trailed off as he slammed the door behind himself.

He strode out to the far side of the driveway, where his little grey Honda civic was parked in the gravel. Nothing fancy, but it was all his. He and his dad picked it out when he turned 16.

He clicked the door open with his key and as he backed out of the driveway he used the opportunity to pull another asshole move. The grass was getting soggy and muddy from the downpours that week, so he purposefully backed out at an angle, so he would be driving through the grass, make a c shape of tire tracks deep and imbedded in the fantastically manicured lawn. This had been the routine for days, creating fresh marks on the grass, now deep cuts from his tires were visible and obvious.

Then, he turned up his music and drifted down the street and towards school.

# CHAPTER 18

Logan treaded through the hall at Hillvale High School, keeping an eye out for Simon as he went. He was Logan's support system. Kept Logan feeling alive, he was mischievous, funny, accidentally insightful and always around when you needed him. Except when he couldn't be found...

They'd been friends since middle school and Simon was the only person he could think of that he'd miss when he went off to college the next year. They always joked that Simon would tag along, but his family couldn't afford tuition, so Simon would have to work a lot, and take out loans. Simon wasn't exactly keen on spending money on his higher education yet. He was the type that didn't know what the next step would be for himself, but he always landed on his feet. Whereas Logan had things planned in his mind, even if he didn't talk about it much.

The pair were relatively inseparable. Always together

on the evenings and weekends; they knew everything about each other without even talking about it.

Like how Simon knew that Logan cried for a whole week when his dad left but he never said anything. Never made fun of his puffy eyes and bad attitude afterwards. Instead he extracted a small bag of weed, a new video game that he swiped from the local Target and a six pack of cokes when he showed up to rescue Logan from pure dysfunction. Or how Logan knew that Simon was ashamed of his family; he always wished he was up to par with everyone else's monetary status. Simon struggled with being on the poorer end of things but pretended not to be. Which is why he got in a lot of arguments and fights with a few choice characters in the school. Not to mention that those same people really liked to poke and prod Simon.

So, it felt natural for him to keep his drooping eyes peeled for his best friend in the fluorescent hallways.

But he didn't often see Simon before the bell rang for their first class because he always seemed to roll in last minute, unless Logan picked him up for school. He was like a character in an 80's movie and always made a big show of things he did. Much unlike Logan, who liked to quietly chuckle under his breath and scoot by without much commentary.

Logan mumbled "hey" to a few buddies in the hallway on his way to his first class. He was in a few advanced classes, Advanced Placement, so he didn't get to spend too many hours with his friends throughout the day. While, it was a bit of a bummer, his classes allowed him to maintain his quieter demeanor, and there weren't as many group projects.

The bell finally rang, causing students to scatter quickly in all directions, like ants. And Logan sauntered to his first class; English.

The one class he actually really enjoyed too. He was able to exercise some form of creativity and chat with a few of the nerdier kids in school too, who always had some extraordinary ideas. He found it refreshing. Plus, he wanted to write, to maybe be a teacher too, or run websites, so this class was something that held his attention more because the content was intriguing to him. Plus, he was always to school on time now because his favorite class kicked off the day.

This morning their teacher rolled in swiftly, briefcase in hand and giant water bottle in the other.

"Hey all, I don't have much planned today besides doing peer edits of your creative stories. Do y'all just want to break out into groups and do those? It's Friday after all, let's keep it simple" he smiled, as he found his seat. He gestured at them with open arms, "Get to it, I'll be wandering around a bit, otherwise, socialize but keep it low key, let's get this shit done!"

Mr. Turner was a cool guy, he had a few books published, he had his masters in writing and literature and he treated the class like they were adults. Like real adults. So, he often turned them loose to do their own thing in class and because of that, everyone was willing to put in the extra work in his class.

Logan spun half around in his seat and half waved at a group of two other guys. One was named Scott, a boisterous drummer in band, who was thought to be gay. Funny dude, not the best writer but was always happy to leave constructive criticism and ask questions.

And the other was a kid named Seth. Quiet, reserved, equipped with loads of technology and was an absolute creative genius, in Logan's humble opinion. If he weren't so damn quiet, Logan would have loved to pick his brain more. Instead of him chatting about his suggestions when evaluating Logan's writing, he would just generate a full page of hand written notes. Full of detail, suggestions, and examples. More than once Logan felt his jaw drop when he read the feedback. *Interesting guy* Logan had thought.

Seth's writing style reminded Logan of an online

account he followed regularly. It was full of illustrations; concise stories, the author never revealed his identity. It was a curious situation, but Logan had become immersed in his work, and more than a few times, he caught himself wondering if the mastermind behind the work was someone similar to Seth. But he couldn't bring himself to ask. The query would only result in laughter and he only half believed his theory anyway. What were the chances of that being true? He just shrugged it off.

The three boys huddled up, twisted their chairs and formed a lopsided circle, or triangle rather. Passed their stories to the right and started reading. Logan glanced up at one point and saw Seth scribbling furiously on his sheet of paper. Seth glanced up, catching Logan's eye, who smirked at him and made a motion with his mind to say, "You're blowing my mind, man". Seth looked embarrassed and flustered but smiled weakly and returned to his notes.

After about 20 minutes, they all looked up at each other.

"Next round?" Scott suggested, brows raised eagerly.

"Sounds good, we're cruising" Logan said and Seth simply nodded and tore another blank page out of his notebook, his pen poised.

They did this for another 20 minutes. Handing their

papers to the rightful owners after and scanned the notes they received.

Scott and Logan chatted a bit about their stories, asked some questions of each other and Seth just fidgeted with this pen in his hands, nodding occasionally. If Logan didn't know better, he'd think that Seth wasn't listening because of his distracted demeanor, but he knew better. Seth was listening intently.

"Any big plans for the weekend?" Scott asked after their discussions dissolved.

"Nothing to note, but I'm sure we'll cause some trouble" Logan said with a small grin.

Scott chuckled, "Well with a friend like Simon, I don't think it's possible to stay *out* of trouble. What about you, Seth?"

"Uh- no. No plans. Just video games, I suppose" he murmured, as he nodded methodically. He had started to sketch a little on the corners of his papers. Logan shifted slightly to see if he could see the style of drawing, but Seth had sensed the move and closed his notebook, protectively.

"Nice, nice! I haven't been playing many video games lately. Guess I got busy with band after school started. But I'll have to get some game suggestions from you one of these days" Scott said, maintaining his friendly and genuine attitude.

"Sure, uh, yeah. Let me know. Happy to suggest" Seth said.

"Right on.... what about you, Scotty?" said Logan.

"Just practice, at this point. With the dance and game next week, we aren't really allowed free time. The drumline is working up a new cadence for and the sticking is really difficult" Scott said, drumming his pointer fingers on the edge of his desk for emphasis.

"I'll bet," the bell interrupted, chiming to say class was over.

"Shit, awesome. Well, see you guys next week. Have a good one" Logan finalized the conversation as Mr. Turner boomed over the class for a few last moments.

"Don't forget, final drafts due next Tuesday! Get some work done this weekend everyone. Don't just party your weekend away.... or do! Have fun!" he hollered as he went back to his emails.

The rest of the morning slipped by, as dull and eventful as normal. Logan turned in assignments and took a few notes. Eagerness emerged just a few moments before the lunch bell. Finally, some reprieve from the slow first half of the day.

Logan slipped down the hall, ordered some lunch and

found himself and Simon a table. No doubt some other guys would plop down next to them at some point. But Logan always made a point of finding them a table, his class before was right by the cafeteria so he had an easier time getting them a good spot.

"Dude, finally Friday. Thank fuck" Logan said, as Simon approached with his meager lunch.

"Yeah, agreed. It's been one hell of a boring day. Just been listening to a lot of complaining," he starts to imitate the girls from first period, "Daddy didn't buy me the right car. It was only 20 thousand dollars instead of 25 thousand. UGH!"

In typical Simon fashion, he latched on to making fun of the well-off bitches in his class.

"You haven't moved past those idiots, yet?" Logan laughed.

"You think I'd be used to it by now. But the bitter animal in me just keeps popping out" Simon replied, "So what do we got cookin' this weekend? There is that party on Saturday at Moe's, you still down?"

"Yeah, that'd be cool. I'm down to do something tonight too, if you just want to chill?" Logan raises his eyebrows in question while polishing off his Gatorade.

"Sure thang. That'd be..." Simon trails and Logan spins

around to see what caught his attention. Lyss Rogers.

Logan starts to laugh, "You, my friend, are ridiculous. Isn't she supposed to be a total bitch? Like, classic mean girl type?"

"I don't know. I don't think so. I feel like when I've interacted with her before she seemed, like, ready to be normal. But then one of her bimbo friends always pops up out of nowhere. Maybe we'll see her this weekend" he smirks and shoves some more chips into his mouth and wipes the crumbs on his knee.

"Yeah, she'll probably be there. But you know she'll be there with Derek" Logan pointed out with raised eyebrows.

Derek was supposedly dating Lyss, but no one could confirm. And he was a total rich asshole.

"That guy is such a douche. And a dick. You see his car?" Simon spun around in his chair to look back to Lyss.

"Douche and a dick, huh? Quite the combo. And dude, quit staring" Logan said, throwing his hands up exasperated, sometimes Simon was so embarrassing, "I did see the car though, to answer your question. It's real nice".

"I want to catch her eye." Simon said, "And yes, the car is ridiculous. I want it. Maybe I'll swipe it"

"Classic weirdo-Simon" Logan chuckled again, always bemused by Simon and his bizarre antics.

Simon just kept his gaze in her direction for another moment or two, and Logan kept on with his food. He chatted a bit with some of their friends who stopped by the table. Agreed to meet up for the party on Saturday and they parted ways.

Lunch was over soon; the two guys took off for class. And while Logan knew Simon was joking about the car, he couldn't help but worry that Simon might go for grand theft auto, like in one of their video games. But ultimately, he shrugged it off.

# CHAPTER 19

Logan zombie-d through the remainder of his school day effortlessly and lazily. He chatted with other students. Homecoming was the big topic of conversation, so he found himself shrugging whenever someone asked him about his plans for the big night. Simon would likely handle any plans they had, Logan didn't really care.

Logan didn't understand what was so "big" and "exciting" about homecoming. It was an excuse for everyone to slather themselves in glitter and face paint, scream loudly during a sporting event they didn't understand and then the next night do it all over again. But the fancy version. Slather yourself with hair gel, squeeze into nice clothes and sweat your ass off in a suit at the school gym. Then drink too much.

*Yeah everyone, real glamorous.*

At the end of the day, he didn't even bother waiting around for his buddies, he took off straight for the parking lot. As he stepped outside, he immediately threw his hood on in an attempt to avoid the rain. Then riffled around in his backpack while walking fishing his car keys out of the bottom. They jingled loudly but seemed to slip out of his fingers every time he thought he got his fingers around them.

He unlocked the car, tossed his backpack into the passenger seat. Turned the car on and sat looking through his phone for a few minutes while the windows defrosted from the steamy body heat he brought in.

*Should have asked Simon if he needed a ride,* he thought, *then again, he likes the rain.*

Flicking quickly through his texts, he noticed a few from his mom letting him know she was happy to make dinner that evening, if he had any requests. One from Simon mentioning getting together and that he'd swing by a little later. An email notification from the college he was interested in letting him know that applications were being accepted. Then he aimlessly scrolled through Instagram.

He internally rolled his eyes at the after-school 'stories' and posts that a bunch of girls had already made; "Friyay!!" they read, as the gals glowed with faux excitement for their pathetic social lives.

Looking up from his phone, he heard a few people pass by his car as they stalked through the lot to find their own vehicles, ducking heads low to avoid getting soaked. The windows had cleared, so he stuck his phone in the middle console, deciding not to respond to his mom, and maneuvered his way out of the parking lot and towards home.

Logan had always loved the drive home. It was relaxing, especially in the fall when the roads were still visible. In the winter they were incredibly dim by 3pm and it made the drive sluggish and a bit nerve-wracking. Today, the leaves fell sloppily from the branches, golden, auburn, crispy and fluttering. Some rain drizzled onto the wind shield.

Logan played a game with himself when he drove in the rain. It didn't have a name, but he would go as long as he could without using his wipers. He would drive, let the water accumulate and then eventually enact the flinging and squeaky wipers as soon as his vision was too blurred.

He didn't do it when anyone else was in the car, but he did it when he was alone.

His house was secluded, so the only danger was hitting an animal, but driving off the road was out of the question. Those roads, winding and deep were his home, he was the most comfortable driving those roads. He smiled to himself slightly as he went around a large corner where the lake could be seen. The rain was letting up, at least for now.

When he pulled up to the house, he plopped down on the porch. The porch was his mother's pride and joy. She had a swing with cushions, and big chairs, flower pots and decor. She would sit out drinking coffee in the mornings in the spring; admiring her beautifully maintained garden.

He flung his backpack near the front door upon his arrival, and rifled through his bag again, before letting it slouch into an indiscernible bundle. He finally found a small baggy of weed, and some rolling papers.

He clumsily rolled up a joint and lit it with a lighter that he kept under one of the posts on the porch. He sat back with this back against a large potted plant, completely protected from the drizzling by the large porch's roof, smoked and let the wind howl around him. The wind chimes tinkling lightly down the way. The rain trickling out of sync constantly, a chill outdoor afternoon.

The tracks in the grass, from his mornings angry escapade was visible from where he sat, the markings were deep. A pang of guilt rose up in him as he thought about his behavior and his mother's texts. She meant well, but forgiveness is hard to provide when everything had been kept so quiet. His mother never vocalized, never told him anything. The silence was the biggest point of contention for Logan. All he wanted was some honesty. At this point, he'd be going to college soon, it's not like he couldn't comprehend the problems of a big, bad adult.

He postulated quietly, and heard his phone vibrate another time inside his bag. He leaned over, careful not to ash on himself, and read the text.

Mom: Hon, I hate to bother, but just let me know what you're plans are tonight, okay? I don't want to worry. We're supposed to have a bit of a storm tonight...so you know...mom stuff.

He took another drag on the now falling apart joint and decided to respond just as a shiny ass car started to pull into the driveway. Logan paused briefly to squint at the car.

"Who the fuck- oh shit" he said out loud and started to stand up, "Dude, what the fuck. No!"

And low and behold, shit head Simon fumbled his way out of *Derek's* car.

"Your chariot awaits, M' Lord" he exclaimed, pompously in a cruddy English accent. He mentioned something about sharing weed, but Logan could barely hear him.

"What. The. Fuck. Dude." Logan stammered as he stuffed his phone into his back pocket, put out his joint under his foot and started towards Simon.

"I thought we could go for a drive?" smiled Simon.

"What are you doing? You fucking idiot. You're going to get arrested!" Logan finally let out a bit of a chuckle as his best friend continued to model ridiculously next to the car of the richest fuck in the school. Holy shit, he committed grand theft auto. Holy shit.

"I'm not. I'll be fine, but that dickhead Derek deserves a bit of a scare. We had a bit of a confrontation after lunch. C'mon....let's take a drive. You got a lighter?"

"You sure man? You know I'd love to piss my mom off right now but getting in serious trouble isn't actually the plan..." he trailed off.

"It'll be fine. If anything, I'll take the fall. All is good. Get in. The seats are warm" he winked and slipped inside the car.

Logan nodded, still completely appalled and exhilarated. He gestured delicately to the house with his thumb, and half jogged to the front porch. He unlocked the front door, tossed his bag inside, made sure his keys were in his pocket. As he made his way back to the car he pulled out his cell and opened his messages with his mom,

> Logan: No worries mom. I'm going to see Si for a bit. I'll be back this evening. Have some work to do when I get home. I'd be okay watching a movie.

She responded as he closed the door.

Mom: Okay, great. Have fun!

His guilt crept up again briefly, until Simon started up the stereo, drowning out his regret.

Logan raised an eyebrow at Simon as they pulled back on to the road and started slipping slowly around the lake. Simon loved this drive about as much as Logan did, and it made Logan happy to share it with his best friend.

They turned the music down quickly and just watched the road as they delved further into the beautiful fall fairytale land. Si sped up and Logan relaxed, the car handled the corners well and he was a surprisingly good driver considering he only ever rode his beat up old bike around town.

After a short jaunt, they started to creep into the parking lot for a spot on the far side of the lake. This was a place where the family went when he was young. They would swim and float and feel like the whole lake was their own because not many people knew about this spot. It had a very "locals only" vibe about the area, and Logan was glad to share its existence with Simon.

They slipped out to the docks, and Simon checked his pockets for cigarettes as they locked up the, now muddy, sports car. Logan flashed him a peek of the lighter in his palm, and they trudged down the narrow path through the water-soaked ground to the docks.

Plopping down, legs stretched out and dangling over the edge of the water. The wind was a bit louder out here and they could watch the trees flutter in the wind across the way.

Simon flipped open the lid of his crumpled pack of cigarettes and handed Logan one, as he stuck one in his mouth and snatched the lighter.

"So, holy shit, this is insane" said Logan after lighting his own and taking a drag.

"Yeah, sorry man. I mean really, I don't want to get you in trouble. But it just felt *right"* Simon responded dreamily, gazing at the water.

Chuckling he responded, "You really are insane, but you know I'm around. Thanks for including me in your bizarre need to cause a commotion".

"Anytime, anytime." he sat quietly for a moment and Logan could feel a serious conversation beginning, "It's just hard, you know. My parents work their asses off. We are broke as fuck. I get shit on for it at school by these well-off pricks and it's just, like, not fair. I know how it is, like *life's not fair* or whatever. But, it's just, not. I just hate those people. That's all".

He fell quiet, starred at his shoes, as he kicked his feet

with the peaceful water glistening in the background. He frowned, the most serious he had been all day. "I'm sorry".

Logan waded in his friend's words, "Don't be sorry. Don't even think about being sorry. You're right. Life isn't fair. It sucks, and good people get the short end of the stick. It's a massive bummer. And sometimes being a rebel vigilante is all you can do"

The boys looked at each other, Simon nodded slowly as he looked back at his feet, kicking his holey Converse wildly, still nodding, face non-descript. He seemed to be thinking heavily.

"At the risk of sounding obsessed with you; you're a great friend. Thanks, man" Simon chuckled and threw his butt into the water.

"Anytime, you're my people, ya know?" Logan muttered back. He put his out too, but left it on the edge of the dock, watching it dance around from the push of the wind.

In an attempt to lighten the conversation Logan said, "So, Lyss fucking Rogers, huh?".

"Yeah, man. She vill be mine" Simon responded in his Dracula voice. "But seriously man, more than meets the eye with that pretty lady. I'm going to get to know her. You mark my words"

"Alright alright, as long as she doesn't ever fuck with game nights, then I'm cool with it", half joking, half serious.

They kept chatting for a while, before Logan checked his phone.

"Hey, man. There is some stuff I gotta do tonight, Mom will be home soon. Mind if we take off?"

"Absolutely, I should get this damn car back anyway. I'm pretty sure I'll be in some shit soon" snickered Simon.

The boys jumped up, as the rain started to thump a little harder on their backs. They shoved their hoods on and beanies down, walking a little faster. The longer they were gone, the longer the car was missing. Logan hoped Simon would be okay.

When they pulled up in front of the house, it was finally dark out. The sun was not lingering around for any play time, like it did in the summer. The lights in Logan's house glowed, the light caressing the tress and dancing flippantly.

They agreed to talk the next day, "if you're not in jail" Logan thought to himself. Waved goodbye and sauntered into the house.

Food was cooking. It smelled wonderful.

"Logan, you home?" his mom sang quizzically from the kitchen, her goofy music playing on her small Bluetooth speaker.

"Yup. The one and only" he said, suddenly happy to hear her voice. "I have a few things to do. I'll eat whatever is left over. That cool?"

"Sure, hon. I'll just stick this in the fridge. Buh-byeeeeeee" she laughed to herself as her pajama-clad self appeared in the doorway. Logan hoped she couldn't see his bloodshot eyes. She winked at him as he half smiled and made his way up the stairs, sweeping his backpack up in the process.

Logan didn't really have any work to do, but he was a bit of an obsessive neat freak, despite his messy and disheveled outward appearance. He liked his thoughts, assignments and next steps to be clear.

Dumping out his notebooks, and quickly reminding himself of what happened in each class that day, be began to get organized. He was serious about school in a nonchalant way, he wanted to go to a good school and was determined to get the grades to make it happen. He made a quick little list on a sticky note of the assignments and work that was due on Monday and stuck it to the edge of his desk.

He flopped down in his swivel chair and clicked his lap top awake. Read through his email about applying to college, scrolled through Facebook (mainly in case he saw any news about Simon getting in trouble) and then navigated to one of his favorite sites. The one that reminded him so heavily of the work that Seth, from English did.

The illustrations that stared out from the screen were tidy but messy and absolutely vibrant. That was the one thing that he didn't know about Seth from his doodles, he never had any color, just smudged pencil drawings, so he couldn't compare Seth's work to the online community. Either way, the drawings were so fun, hilarious and could be scathingly relatable.

He noticed there was a new post.

It depicted a teenager in a crib (who in Logan's opinion resembled Seth), with his head tucked between his knees, as if crying, as a cloud of smoke wafted through the air overhead, suggesting drug use. Then a smattering of people, whose heads were distorted and covered by the billowing fumes, to save their identity from being revealed. They had speech bubbles poking out, hauntingly with things that said, "loser", "friendless", "who are you?" etc. It was a haunting and vulnerable illustration.

In that moment, Logan felt deeply for the artist, whoever it may be and decided to say something about it. After listening to Simon that afternoon, Logan felt like communication just became the biggest and most important thing he could do. He furiously and thoughtfully wrote out:

"Hey man. I'm a big fan of your work. I don't know how many people send you these messages, so maybe this will get lost among your comments and messages, but I figured I'd say something anyway.... I have my fair share of problems, trust me. And my best friend is a bit of a mess right now too. I just want you to know that there are so many people out there who look up to you, enjoy your work and want to see you continue. So, whatever's going on in your life, I hope that it doesn't keep you from living your best life. Sorry if this is kind of cheesy, but I'd want to hear it if I felt alone. That's what friends are for, and this online community is full of your friends. 'Night man. Good luck".

He hesitated on clicking the send button. *Jesus I sound like a dweeb,* he thought, but sighed and thought, *if my art spoke to someone, I'd want to know too* and clicked 'Send' quickly before he could take it back.

He snapped his sleek laptop shut and zipped into his bathroom for a quick shower, mainly to wash away the smell of cigarettes and pull on his sweats and favorite sweatshirt his dad bought him.

He looked around his room, studying his belongings. Stalking over to the small stash of airplane shot bottles and stuffed 5 or 6 into his pocket. He smiled to himself, *sure why not.*

Padding down the stairs, where Karen was watching a movie that she had rented on the massive, cozy ass couch.

"Whatcha watching?" he says cheerfully as he sees the movies villain pull out a knife and start to sneak up on a scantily glad, pretty woman with perfect blond hair.

His mother loved thriller and horror films. The lights were dim, a few small lamps on. She spun around quickly.

"Jesus, you're swift as the goddam night. You scared the hell out of me" she smiled, as she touched her hand to her chest in feign scared motion. A glass of wine balanced in her other hand, she was wrapped in blankets and had pillows tucked under her arms. "Go. Get some food. Come join me".

After filling his plate, he snagged two sodas from the fridge and went to join his mom.

"Really looking for a sugar rush, huh?" she smiled at him, gesturing at the sodas.

He cracked open his soda, took a swig, reached inside his pocket uncapped a small Captain Morgan's and dumped it into his soda. He looked up at her bemused, she looked shocked. Then quickly unsurprised, as she started to laugh. He smiled back.

"Are you fucking kidding me, kid? I know you drink and do so safely, but right in front of me without permission?

You're certainly getting away with a lot" she stuck out her left hand, opened her palm and gestured that he hand another bottle over to her.

She opened one up and took a drink from the miniature bottle.

"Damn, mom. Get down with it" Logan laughed.

"Your mom knows how to drink, I just hide it with these nasty, classy bottles of Cab" she smirked back at him as he handed her the other soda. She leaned forward and ditched the wine on the coffee table. They laughed for a few minutes, just simply joking. Then launched into an actual conversation. Touching on school, on work, on college, friends and so on. It was the first real conversation they'd had in months. And it was refreshing.

Logan's mom told some stories about her high school days and trailed off finally when she started a story with, "One time, your dad and I...."

They both went quiet, smiles slid off their faces, silence rang.

"Um, mom?" Logan said, brow furrowed.

"Yeah, hon..." she said distractedly, staring down at her empty left hand. She was tracing the lip of the can with her pointer finger, not letting herself make eye contact.

"Can we talk about this whole thing? I... I guess I just

feel bad. I know I've been pretty shitty to live with since Dad took off, but part of that is because no one will tell me the story. I don't even know what happened" he glanced up at her.

Her eyes were filled with tears and she was looking right at him. Completely sobered.

"I just...never wanted to make your father the bad guy. I didn't want to be the bad guy either. I thought you didn't want to know about it. I don't know why, I just...this is so difficult. I didn't want you to be my shoulder to cry on. I'm the adult, I wanted to continue to be that" she responded, shivering and sipping.

"Mom, no. I just want the honest truth. I love you both. I want to get along with you. Get along with Dad, but he hasn't come back. He doesn't talk to me. I just want to know why. I feel like I've blamed you and I don't think that's fair of me" he said firmly. He felt awkward about it, so he took another drink.

He looked at his mother, again. She wiped a tear away, smiled and nodded.

"Okay, hon, you're right. You deserve the truth. You're old enough to know that we both love you and I understand your need to know. Let's talk about it" she said.

She pulled her thick, dark hair into a loose hair tie, and

gestured for another airplane shooter, "I'll need another drink please" and chuckled.

She just sat the shooter on the table and turned to face Logan.

They spent the next few hours crying together, talking together and drinking together.

# PART SIX

*Jay*

# CHAPTER 20

The mornings weren't the part of the day that excited Jay the most. He'd wake up, rolled out of bed and slump through his room and fiddling on his phone. He'd crank some music on Spotify and try not to roll his eyes for the entire morning, while he got ready. It was a struggle, though.

His bedroom was covered in decorations. An obvious amount of planning and time had gone into the décor and layout.

Polaroid photos filled the wall above the faux wooden desk from Pottery Barn and twinkly lights were draped casually over the bedframe of the same white washed, drift wood color. A tapestry of swirling creams and blues hung perfectly over the bed too. There was a large bookshelf near the closet door that was packed with novels, colorful coffee table books and a middle shelf full of framed photos, a small banner that said "Happy Birthday Jay-Bae-Bae" with small notes and cards from his friends perched on it. The room was bright, modern and cozy. Exactly the way he had envisioned it.

Jay stalked down the hallway in flannel pajama pants and a Stranger Things t-shirt, toward the bathroom he shared with his younger sister, Tiffany.

She had, per usual, already claimed the bathroom and barricaded herself inside. The door locked and steam issuing from the crack under the door like the set of a bad music video.

Jay rapped his fist loudly on the door attempting to be heard over the sound of the shower and the shrill voice of Tiff belting the words to the newest Halsey song, which was about as sad and pathetic as his sister was herself. His sigh of frustration echoed down the hall, he certainly excelled in dramatics.

"Tiffany. Get out of the shower! My turn," Jay said sternly and loudly, glaring at the victimized wooden door that separated the bickering siblings.

"WHAT? I"M IN HERE . . . HELLO?" she screamed back, and he could hear her snickering knowingly.

*Ah, yes. The age-old trick. Pretend you can't hear anything over the water.*

"CHRIST, TIFF" Jay shouted at full volume, as he tipped his head against the back of the door in defeat. "For fucks sake" he mumbled before sounding off in the direction of his folks' room.

"Parents! This is why we need another bathroom, I'm going to school smelling like a teenage boy again!!!"

His blonde, petite mother poked her head out of the door with a smile stretched across her lined, but pretty face. Her hair propped up on top of her head, and a blouse hanging from her small frame.

"That's why we buy you cologne, right?" and stuck her tongue out and disappeared again to finish getting ready for work.

Jay smiled and rolled his eyes and banged on the door to the bathroom one more time before retreating back to his bedroom. Truth be told, he showered the night before, so it wasn't that big of a deal, but still. It was the principle of thing was what bothered him. Plus, the dramatics.

He slipped into some Bieber-esque joggers, a camo jacket and pulled a hat on backwards over his well-maintained, short dark hair. Rustling around in the top drawer of his dresser, he found his deodorant and a bottle of cologne, that he purposefully left in his bedroom for these instances. Lesson learned, really.

Clothing had always been relatively important to Jay. It wasn't like, his main thing. He wasn't obsessed, but his mother regularly joked about how he liked to "look good" always. Which wasn't false, it just seemed like an odd thing for her to hold on to. There was nothing wrong with established your personal style, right?

Jay wasn't in to sports, per se. But he did like to stay involved at school. He was ASB Secretary, he liked design so creating posters for events was his jam. And he ran sprints in the spring with Track and Field. Running wasn't an extracurricular he initially thought he'd enjoy. He started one year when his mom encouraged him to try something new.

Now he would go on long jogs through his neighborhood throughout the year to stay in shape and to burn off some stress.

Grades weren't an issue for Jay, he kept his GPA high and managed to keep up with hobbies. The deal with the folks was that if he was involved at school then he didn't need to get a job. It was a nice deal, but some extra spending money would have been nice.

But it wasn't the worst problem he could have, and it wasn't the most challenging problem that existed for him.

In fact, Jay was gay.

It wasn't a problem, per se. But it hadn't been acknowledged by any family or friends yet. It's not like someone was going to ask, right?

He had never even said it out loud. "I'm gay" hadn't stumbled out of his mouth before. But he assumed people suspected his sexuality wasn't exactly on the straight and narrow.

It took him quite a while to admit this exclusive fact, even to himself. It's not like he hadn't tried dating or hadn't had girlfriends. He certainly had little flings, but all those gals ended up being some of his friends. And the breakups had always been mutual.

He finally came to terms with his sexuality when he went to a leadership camp with ASB two summers earlier. He had met a new friend from a school in Canada. It was an international camp, maybe sixty schools were invited to participate. The camp basically encouraged students to learn about different ways to operate as a student body government, wanted students to get excited about diversity and get to know people from different areas and how they live. A big ol' diversity, leadership shindig.

They ended up partnering schools up together from different sides of the country. There were discussions and games and trust fall's galore.

That's when Jay met Danny.

Danny had short, light hair, pale skin. He was medium height, stocky but wholly attractive. And, much to Jay's surprise Danny befriended Jay quickly. He latched on, actually. Jay remembered being surprised and assumed Danny just wanted to be buddies. In fact, Jay didn't think that Danny was gay at the time either. Danny had a handful of guy friends, an Instagram page full of sporting events and pretty girls under his arm for homecoming and so on. The typical signs weren't there. But, Jay supposed he didn't flaunt any signs either. Up until that summer he was completely unaware and possibly in denial.

The guys had a similar sense of humor, despite their vastly different interests. They became friends anyway. Opposites attract, or whatever. That's how it started and Jay didn't have any reason to think anything otherwise. The only weird part of their new-found friendship was the way that Jay's palms would begin to sweat, chest would pound harder when he heard Danny's voice.

Over the week at camp, a bunch of people buddied up with other schools. They made "best friends" with students on the other side of the country and promised to be pen pals. They promised to keep in touch on Facebook (which of course, they forgot those promises as soon as they got home).

Like everyone else, Jay and Danny were attached at the hip. They were opposites in almost every way. Danny liked super hero movies and listened to 90's rap and hip hop.

Whereas Jay had a faux obsession with Wes Anderson and preferred to listen to Lorde, belting the lyrics into his cell phone, pretending it was a mic, followed by bursts laughter.

But they could laugh together. And on one of the last nights of camp, the whole population of attending students got together for one last movie night. They piled into the mess hall with blankets, cozy clothes and pillows to watch a multitude of cheesy, classic teen films together before departing the next day. The last big night of bonding and laughs.

On the final night, everyone snuggled in on the floor and miscellaneous thrift store couches and chairs. Danny and Jay ended up sitting closely together, packed in tight leaning against a large squishy love seat. Sardined with the other students and half way through the movie Wet Hot American Summer, Danny slowly inched his fingers on to Jay's leg. Right above his knee. And, out of shock, Jay spun his head sideways, almost fast enough to crack his lean neck. Danny had his eyes on the screen but was grinning ear to ear, he glanced at Jay from the corner of his eye and winked slyly.

Jay smiled too. His face heated up, his palms sweat and he felt tingles going up his spine. A nervousness and need he hadn't felt before with any girl.

After the movie, most of the campers skipped to the

mess hall to get a pile of chocolate, graham crackers and marshmallows, then rushed to the fire pit. Jay and Danny instead took a walk.

Nothing particularly intense happened. They walked quietly, their fingers slipping playfully around each other's, little serpents, dancing around and around.

At one point, Danny turned to Jay looking apologetic.

"I'm sorry that this can't be more, I don't know, real? But you have really opened my eyes, Jay. I hope we can remain friends after this summer. I need to figure out how to make my life real in this lifestyle. But a lot of people aren't going to be happy about it. I hope you understand..." he trailed off.

"I understand" Jay had mumbled, "My folks are crazy supportive of everything I do, but there is something about coming out to them and feeling like you've been lying to them and yourself for so long. I've never been able to admit this to even myself, either".

This was the first time Jay was able to acknowledge that he was gay, and the realization hit him suddenly and filled him with clarity. With Danny, he didn't feel embarrassed.

Danny nodded sympathetically, and they continued walking in silence before turning around to the join the others.

Danny, before parting ways ended their fling with, "Let's stay in touch. I'm busy back home, but I hope we can talk" and planted a small, delicate kiss on Jay's cheek before giving him a polite hug and stalking off, hands in pockets back to where his school mates were gathered and joking loudly.

Jay had stood there, in silence, half smiling, half sad. Watching Danny's stocking figure hunch towards his schools group, where everyone slapped him on the back and laughed loudly at his arrival. Jay finally went to also join some of his best friends in their circled-up group.

They stayed in touch initially, but both got lazy, stopped caring maybe, and eventually, they didn't talk at all.

But if anything, Jay could now admit to himself, even if he couldn't admit to anyone else, that he was, in fact, gay.

If anything, his biggest give away wasn't that he hadn't *had* girlfriends, it was more that all of his *actual* friends were girls. He felt like a stereotype in that way. He had dude friends, but they weren't the people he made plans with on the weekends, they were the people he had group projects with and joked with in class and interacted with when he was in full face paint at the football games. But not, spend-the-night-and-play-video-games-all-night kinds of friends.

Jay was loud, very funny and liked to know about everything.

He finished packing up his backpack, gave himself the once over in his floor length mirror that was bordered with wire lights. He raised an eyebrow at himself, before pulling on his hat and strode out of his room.

As he stepped into the hall, Tiffany emerged from the bathroom at the same time, full face of makeup, hair perfectly perched on her petite shoulders. She stuck her tongue out, as he slipped into the bathroom to brush his teeth quickly. On his way out the front door he decided to shout one last angry insult at his little sister.

"BYE!" He shouted, full force, "HOPE YOU GET AS SOAKED AS YOU DID IN YOUR SHOWER ON THE WAY TO SCHOOL", he chuckled while his mom laughed mercilessly from the kitchen.

"That'll teach her!" his mom hollered back and Jay grinned, happy that his parents participated in the joke.

Loping down the front porch towards his car, he hears a cat call from across the road.

"Lookin' fuckin' snazzy Miss Thang" Sierra exclaims, her thick curly hair engulfing her thin face.

She smiles quickly and gestures towards the car,

"How's your morning?"

"Ugh, fine. I'm tired as hell though. I don't know how you do all of this! You're so damn organized and you somehow still manage to look like a goddess for school every morning! Not to mention, I couldn't shower. Goddam sister was belting some bullshit song this morning and steaming up the place without my ability to invade."

Jay rolled his eyes dramatically and unlocked his car.

"Oh, gosh. Don't even. You have no idea. Either way, let's get going. I've got some info to file before class starts" she says as they both slide into his little two door beater and gently drift down the cul-de-sac and head to school.

# CHAPTER 21

Sierra wiggles her long, skinny fingers at Jay as she propels herself out of the barely parked car to run in to the school. Smiling over her shoulder, as she heads off to hide in the ASB lounge.

Jay had grown up with Sierra, they'd been neighbors since childhood. And just as she was the one person who likely knew Jay was gay, he was the one person who had noticed Sierra's weight dropping steadily since 10th grade. Since she began stressing. He always said nice things about how she looked. Jay would be the first to admit she was stunning, she was a champion, nothing wrong with that. But sometimes he felt guilty. Like he was perpetuating her bad habits. He tried to convince himself that if he said nice things about her, she would see that she is strong and beautiful without shoving her fingers down her delicate little throat. He was all ears whenever she wanted to talk about problems or frustrations, he always encouraged her to eat, as subtlety as he could muster. Subtlety wasn't his strongest trait.

He honestly didn't know what the best option was, anymore. And they didn't hang out as much as they used to. So, he didn't consider it his responsibility to take care of her. She should know better.

He sighed heavily as he bopped in to school after locking up his dopey little car. He slung his backpack over one shoulder and started dodging rain puddles on his way across the lot.

The walls surrounding the lockers were plastered in homecoming posters already, but more would be added. School spirit was incredibly prominent at Hillvale.

A few girls hollered at him as soon as he spun around from his locker. One of his best friends, Becca wiggled her fingers at him. Her long colorful hair flung behind her back, her book bag dangling from her arm and cell phone clutched tightly in her hand. She was an attractive, bubbly girl with unique style and a busty chest, attention wasn't something she had to work too hard for.

Winking at Becca and giving her a side hug, she and Jay immediately started to gossip like a bunch of old hens.

"Oh. Shit! I forgot, did you hear??" Becca squeaked, as she tossed her freshly dyed hair behind her shoulder and her eyes widened. This was the expression that usually became plastered to her face when she had something juicy to spill.

"Uh-no. Wait hear about what? You need to be more specific, Becs" Jay spat back at her.

"Sorry, sorry. I know that. I just got so excited"

"Oooo-kay. Well spit it out already" Jay said, his annoyance covered by his excitement. Becca wasn't exactly the brightest crayon in the box.

"Right, right. So, you know Scott? The drummer in the drumline. Broad, cute face, glasses and like really nice hair?" she whispered loudly.

"Yeah, 'course I know Scott" Jay mumbled back, half listening, but his interest piqued.

"Well, apparently he came out to his family and friends and is like fully gay now. He's telling his friends now" Becca finished excitedly bouncing on the balls of her feet.

"What?" Jay spun to face her, "Seriously? Whoa."

"Yeah, crazy right? Like, so brave of him! And apparently the whole school is being, like, hella cool about it"

"Hm- interesting" Jay said, envy rising in his chest. "Well, I got to go. I have some stuff to organize before class".

And before Becca could respond, he took off for his first period classroom.

The room was still empty, classes didn't begin for

another ten minutes. So, he savored the silence and pulled up Scott's social media profiles on his sleek cell phone, nothing had changed on the accounts. Everything looked the same.

Despite the lack of changed, Jay scrolled through his photos, admiring his large, genuine smile. His teeth shining in each photo. Scott was handsome. No denying it.

All of the photos were of Scott and some band members, repping the school colors and making silly faces.

He frowned and felt pissed. He slid the accounts closed and glared at the clock.

*Why does this happen? I am way too much of a pussy to come out, this guy does it and is praised. Brave?? Seriously? I don't want the attention, I just want my friends and family to accept me.... I can't even begin to think about how to approach such a situation. And Scott is such a douche, he's always so damn happy. Whatever, he doesn't deserve to have it easy.... he was already a happy guy.*

Tears welled up in his eyes without warning and he quickly wiped them away. The bell rang and students began to trickle into the room. Forcing attention elsewhere to avoid tears from streaming, he reached into his bag and pretended to be a diligent note taker for once.

Jay didn't have any classes with Scott, but he sure thought about him all day.

The green beast was taking control. Annoyance and jealously engulfed Jay as he reflected on his inability to be courageous enough to come out. Truthfully, Jay was terrified of the change that may follow such an announcement. Would they treat him different? Treat him like a liar? Would the jokes change? Would people tippy toe around him?

He didn't want boys from childhood who he changed with at the pool to accuse him of being a creep. He didn't want to become someone's GBF and be forced to go clothes shopping or some shit with Becca. He didn't want to be pigeon holed by his closed-minded school into being a stereotype. Jay knew himself, and he knew if they forced a thing on him, he would give in and be that person.

He huffed his way through the rest of the day.

Sitting with Becca and the crew at lunch, munching quietly on carrot sticks and slurping down a soda as he shoved a sandwich into his face, Jay completely ignored all conversation. He decided to stop by Sierra's table to confirm the ASB meeting meet up for after school. The chore gave him something to do for a few minutes, a distraction. He slowly began to daydream about running in to and confronting Scott.

He didn't know what he would say, but he knew he wanted to confront him. Blind with anger, Jay planned to track Scott down and give him the third degree. Scott would be the target for Jay's frustration and anger.

*Why am I so adamant about this? I feel obsessed. I'm shaking with rage right now. I just feel like Scott should know that he is making life difficult for others.*

Jay had convinced himself that Scott was the enemy, in his own story.

The rest of the day went by quickly, it always did for Jay on Friday's because he was usually 100% not committed to any learning on the eve of the weekend.

The day finally ended, and Jay had a hard time holding conversations with any one after school. He listened to Becca squeak at him for about ten minutes before turning to her and saying, "Look Becs, I love you. But I am kind of in a funk and I'm not taking in anything you're saying"

She gaped at him briefly before responding, "It's okay. I was just explaining the anatomy hot pockets to you, so it's not that big of a deal".

Jay rolled his eyes violently, sighing hard in Becca's direction. She shrugged and smiled her small twinkly little smile and skipped down the hall saying, "I'll text ya later, babe!"

Now even more annoyed because of Becca's positivity, he glowered at everyone in his path. Trying to pull himself together before an intimate group hang out with all of the ASB kids.

Jay stalked to the ASB room, where the whole crew had gathered, talking excitedly about the homecoming dance the following week and waited for Sierra and Mr. G to show up and boss them around. Well, G never bossed, he made jokes and let Sierra run the show. But still.

Jay rubbed his temples and decided internally to turn his attitude around before dealing with everyone. Being the center of attention and joking around might cheer him up.

*It's not good for anyone to be negative and shitty. Just buck up and deal, you idiot. Pull your head out of your ass.*

He slapped a smile on his long face and waltzed into the middle of the group.

"Alright people!" he said smiling and tugging Sierra into the middle of the circle, where everyone gathered up as she rolled up. "Our Queen has arrived, and the pizza line is open for business. Please, please listen to the woman and let's get this shit done so we can wrap up for the weekend!"

The entire group cheered and whooped while Mr. G smiled and lazily said, "Language".

The ASB officers split up in to groups and started to design a bunch of decorations, signs, posters. Everyone had plates full of steaming pizza slices.

The group munched away loudly, cheese and sauce flying all over the circular table. As the evening got a little further on, Jay noticed Sierra shovel almost three full pieces of delicious pizza pie into her mouth and he smiled to myself, proud that she was making some effort.

He got to chatting again with some younger members, where more people gossiped about Scott and Jay didn't comment but listened intently.

"Yeah apparently his mom is single, his dad passed a few years back, but she was super chill with it. He told some people that he owed it to himself to be honest with everyone in his life even if they didn't like his lifestyle, or some shit. But still, good for him".

The conversations continued like this.

*Great, so if I come out, will people think I'm just hopping on the bandwagon? I am an attention whore, so I'm sure some people will assume I'm just being a jackass.*

Jay kept thinking, eyebrows meeting in the middle, until Mr. G finally spoke up.

"Ahem" he said, clearing his throat, "Now, I know you all would just *love* to be at school all night. But I have other plans, and none of those plans involve you snot-nosed kids" he chuckled, "So let's pack this stuff up and pick back up on Monday. And don't forget, it's pajama day on Monday, be as lazy as you please!"

A kid in the sophomore year jokes, "What you got a pretty lady and a six-pack waiting for you at home, Mr. G?"

"As a matter of fact, I don't" he laughs, "I have a wedding to attend tomorrow though, so I need my beauty sleep".

Everyone cleaned up their supplies, washed their paint brushes and shoved their rulers into the cabinets. Dusting off their knees and elbows after laying on the dusty floor for hours.

Jay glances around for Sierra, he wanted to offer her a ride, but she's nowhere in sight.

*Fuck. She's disappeared after eating.... Great.*

She strolls around the corner, eyes wide just moments later straightening her stylish top down.

"Hey, you want a ride?" Jay says, sidling up next to Sierra who seemed jumpy.

"Oh, no. No, thanks. My mom was going to get me, so we could go run some errands".

"On a Friday?" Jay questions, but feeling relieved, not wanting to interrupt his plan to find Scott.

"Uh-yeah. Just a few things before homecoming and she wanted to run to Target, which I never say no to!" she said, trying to save face.

Jay frowns, then decides to smile. Not worth the negativity!

"Okay, sounds good. I'll catch you later" and he tosses his bag on again and speed walks down the far hall in the direction of the band room.

The music has stopped at this point and Jay whispers *"fuck fuck fuck"* under his breath as he speeds down the hall in hopes of running into Scott. The big metal school door slammed open and three guys chatting loudly as they trekked down the hall. Donned with large instruments balanced upon their sides or backs. Luckily, Scott is among the group and the only person not balancing any instruments on his body.

Jay slows down immediately. Holding his breath, relief flooding him. He hadn't missed Scott after all. Slowing down to almost a full stop and staring at his phone, Jay pretends to read a text slowly and with concern, so he can be closer to the exiting group of musicians.

Jay sees Scott glance behind them when he hears Jay's sneakers squeak lightly on the floor, at his abrupt halt.

"Hey guys, I forgot my sticks in the band room, I'll catch y'all later, alright?"

"Sure man! Have a good weekend, maybe hit that party tomorrow, yeah? It's at Moe's. I'll text you" and the other two guys exchange fist bumps with Scott.

"Bye"

Scott turns around slowly, hands in pockets and Jay stops dead. They make eye contact, both boys stopped fully in the empty hall.

"Hi Jay!" he smiles knowingly, pulling a hand out of his pocket to give a wave and pulling his drums sticks out of his back pocket.

"Wait, I thought you forgot your sticks?" Jay spat, glaring now.

"Ah, so you were eavesdropping. I didn't, but I saw you practically sprinting down the hall and then slow down to a complete stop when you saw us. I assumed you wanted to talk to me?" Scott smiled again.

He wasn't mad, confused, or creeped out or anything.

"I don't need anything" Jay retorts and immediately regrets his shitty attitude.

"Alright, man. Suit yourself. Have a good weekend, Jay" and he spins on his heel and continues walking down the hall as he hums loudly and snaps the beat on his right hand.

Jay stares after, admiring his stature, his stride and his ability to be comfortable in his skin.

*His friends didn't even give a shit that he was gay. They didn't even bat an eyelash at making plans with him for the weekend.*

"Wait" Jay shouts.

Scott stops mid step, shimmies his shoulders and says, "Catch up" and continues walking.

Jay jump steps and jogs smoothly to meet up with Scott.

DOWN THE PRIMROSE PATH

# CHAPTER 22

The night is thick as they bust through the big school doors. Walking quietly through the parking lot, Jay trailing behind, holding the straps of his backpack, with Scott bouncing good spiritedly a few steps ahead.

Jay glares at the back of his head, a little annoyed with himself. *This isn't how I expected this interaction to go.*

"Let's go get some ice cream" Scott says, assuredly and self-confident. The frustration he already felt mounted. Jay wasn't about to say no to ice cream with a cute boy, but he didn't like that Scott knew he wouldn't say no.

"What if I don't have time for that?" Jay says, crossing his arm defiantly, even though he is already salivating at the prospect of going to Honey Bears Ice Creamery downtown.

"You have time, or else you wouldn't be walking with me still" he says flashing a smile over his shoulder, which sends a small wave of chills over Jay's body. He shakes the feeling away quickly remembering after a moment he isn't supposed to be happy with Scott.

"I'll drive, if that's cool with you?" Scott continues after the pause, pulling car keys off his belt loop.

"Sure..." Jay responds, suspiciously.

They navigate through the dark parking lot, dodging rain drops as they begin to fall more quickly. Scott motions delicately toward his small hatchback and unlocks the doors quickly and tosses his bag into the backseat. Jay hesitates momentarily, wondering to himself if he really wants to go down this road. Then tugs lightly on the handle and ducks into the car, as well.

While buckling his belt and situating his bag between his knees, Scott fumbles absently with his phone and plugging it in to his car stereo, clearly a new addition to the otherwise plain vehicle. The lights lining the numbers and the dials glow purple, then blue and so on, rotating through the spectrum. Jay sits quietly, rubbing his hands on his thighs, warming up from the chilled rain that splashed them on their expedition across the parking lot.

"I assume you don't want to rock out to some Buddy Rich or Elvin Jones, so how about something newer-ish? Do you like Elderbrook?" Scott asks in earnest, smiling as he looks up at Jay.

"Uh, I don't know. I think I've heard the name, but I'm

not great with matching artists to song titles..." Jay stammered, confused by the simple question while his mind raced. He wasn't planning on discussing his favorite songs, he was simply triggered by his envy and jealousy.

Scott was calm, cool and collected. Like being gay hadn't changed anything in his life.

"Totally. I literally just picked a random song from a Spotify playlist, so I don't know it either" he laughed.

Jay gave a feeble smile.

"Jay, I won't bite. You can relax a little bit. I hope I'm not making you uncomfortable?"

"I'm fine" Jay spat, snatching his hat and looking out of the passenger window.

"Alright" Scott said putting his hands up, "Let's get to it, then"

They drove out of the lot and towards the downtown area. Where the city was littered with numerous shops, boutiques (some small, some large), bookstores, restaurants and a handful of classy bars. But classy didn't always describe their patrons.

Scott navigated them expertly down the busy streets, tapping his thumbs along the steering wheel and adjusting the volume knob constantly. It was obvious to Jay when Scott was intrigued by a specific moment in a song because he would start to nod emphatically and reach for the dial to knock the sound up a few more levels. Bouncing his head rhythmically, scrunching his face tightly attempting to discern the beat through the numerous messy sounds, fake instruments and wailing that was modern indie/pop music.

Jay had the urge to laugh and tease Scott but wasn't completely comfortable. The emotions that waded in his chest confused him. Jay recognized the jealousy, but the pangs of urgency and longing confused him.

Scott glided into a cramped parking spot, Jay felt like he was beginning to lose sight of the goal of this outing though. Should he really feel angry? Envious and furious? Is it really fair for him to feel this? Was he really so angry that someone else was happy and outed when he wasn't? Why should that hurt him?

Jealously and envy made him irrational and quick to decision. As those few minutes in the car ticked away, Jay became increasingly aware of his misinterpretation of his emotions. Loneliness and a separation from his classmates had been a standard feeling in day to day life, and maybe the longing he felt was the need for some companionship. To be around someone who understood, who had similar experiences, who trudged through unknown waters too.

Jay didn't want to overshadow or piggy back on Scott's

decision to come out, but the need to talk about it was becoming increasingly necessary. Vulnerability disguised itself as anger and Jay fought to push that aside.

His life change or admittance would mean more people with stories, more people who would either be shocked, or not. It seemed like more of a social risk than Scott admitting his sexuality. Scott had only lived in Hillvale for a few years. Whereas Jay grew up in the town, and no doubt, some people would call him a liar or think he was a creep.

"All good to go?" Scott said, as he unclipped his belt and started to lower the volume in the car, all nestled into a tight parking spot.

"Yeah" Jay said cautiously, feeling a little bit guilty.

"Cool, les' go" and he slipped into the rain and bounded to the sidewalk across the street and stood under an awning, waiting for Jay to catch up.

"You really don't like to wait around for people, do you?" Jay mumbled, half out of amusement, half from annoyance after he got caught in his seat belt and had to suck in severely to squeeze out of the car because the parking spot was so tight. His sweatshirt was now wet on his back from rubbing on the car.

Scott chuckled, "I guess I could have been more chivalrous, huh?"

*Chivalrous. Was this some kind of "more than friendly"
situation?*

Scott walked closely to Jay. Their shoulders grazed each other's briefly. Jay stared at the ground as they turned the corner.

"I got it" Scott said and galloped quickly to the door of Honey Bear's to open it for Jay. Jay raised an eyebrow at him and smiled.

"Ah, there is the makeup chivalry"

"Yes, my liege".

*Oh my god. Are we flirting? If we run in to anyone, will they
think this is a date?*

They were immediately overcome with the smell of warm waffle cones, sugar and coffee. Honey Bears was the best local joint for sweet treats and nice conversations over a steaming (or iced) cup of caffeine. Jay closed his eyes and breathed in deeply.

"Holy shit. It smells so good" Jay sighed.

"Right? This is the place I'll miss most when we eventually graduate and get the hell out of here. Best place for homework and people watching" Scott motioned for the corner booth and the guys made their way to it, not only the best seat in the house, but one of the only empty tables.

Families were milling about with their kids, getting a

few scoops of ice cream to celebrate the weekend and a few community college students gazing into books and slapping away on some laptops, doing some evening studying before they drank away the rest of their brain cells for the rest of the weekend.

A small, mousy girl with half of her head shaved came over to take their order.

"Hello, hello Scott. Fancy seeing you here" she smiled through her piercings and heavy eyeliner.

"Hi Jenny! Yeah, I know. Fridays aren't usually my standard. Can I get a big ol' cup of drip coffee and a Coffee Chip scoop in a waffle bowl?" Jay said without opening the menu, drooling like a dog.

"Wow, you know what you like!" Scott laughed, "I'll do the same on the coffee but get me a regular bowl of cookie dough?"

She smiled quickly, "Sure thing boys!" and stalked away. Her dark tights and short skirt getting a few glares from a mom or two with their kids.

Scott smiled and starred at a young boy who was covered in ice cream, his dad trying to control his squirming enough to wipe him clean of the sticky mess.

"Soooo-" Scott started, finally looking at Jay directly in the face. Looking slightly amused and raised his eyebrows in anticipation. Waiting for Jay to explain his reasoning for the near attack in the hallway.

"Soo-what?" Jay shot back, his voice settling quickly into a joking manner. The atmosphere was certainly calming him down, letting him see a bit clearer. He nerves calmed and guilt settled into his chest, but Honey Bears was his happy place, so he felt better.

*Scott's not the bad guy, here. You can't be mad at someone for being honest. Maybe this is a lesson for me.*

"How's your school year treating you? I'm sure you're particularly busy right now, with Homecoming next week" Scott said.

"Yeah, actually. It's been a bit nutty. I think the crew is killing it though. The underclassmen have really stepped up to the plate and Sierra just has this down to a science, really" Jay started to nestle into the conversation of regular daily life.

"It seems like it. She is, like, really nice, but man, you can see the stress just seeping from her pores" Scott responded, and looked up to see Jay's shocked face.

His brow furrowed immediately, "Oh, shit. I'm sorry. I know you're good friends with her. I'm not trying to be rude, I guess I just noticed she wears her heart on her sleeve, which, no offense, seems to be getting looser and looser?"

"No, no. You're not being offensive. I worry about her

too. I've just never heard anyone else ever acknowledge that she may have a problem out loud, you know?" he stammered in response.

"Is that what you're worried about? I got the impression you really wanted to talk to me. I'm not sure why.... unless it's about the new 'drama' about me" he said, with air quotes around drama and smirked.

"Uhmmm-" Jay sputtered.

And luckily the punk waitress Jenny arrived at that moment, saving Jay from needing to respond yet. A tray balanced on her shoulder with their mugs of joe and bowls of cream.

"Here y'all are. Let me know if you need anything else, you know where to find me" she smiled in a small, exhausted way.

The boys chimed their 'thanks' and dug in to their ice cream as their coffees cooled to a drinkable temperature.

Jay couldn't stop thinking about what he should respond with and finally worked up the courage between slurps of ice cream and coffee.

"Okay," licking the spoon one last time for good measure, "So, it's true then? You're gay?"

"Yup. Totally true. I have known, of course. But it finally felt like the right time to say something. I didn't want to go through my last years in high school trying to hide anything. I want to leave for college with, like, self-confidence and whatever. I don't know. It seemed like the right time. I'm happy to have told everyone, though. Why do you ask?" he raised one side of his mouth in a half smile, slightly bashful.

Jay looked into his coffee mug and swirled his spoon in it, contemplating. Scott seemed so honest, so open and willing to talk about it. Jay wanted to have that confidence but didn't know if he could make the words leave his mouth. Before he could think about it for another second he quietly said it.

"I'm gay, too" he finally muttered.

Scott intertwined his fingers on the table and looked at Jay in the most serious way he had all night.

"You haven't talked about this before?" he responded, quietly and carefully.

"No. No, I haven't ever really said it out loud"

Tears had welled up in his eyes without his permission and he pushed his thumbs into his tear ducks. Trying to stop the flow, to avoid the embarrassment. His chest heaved a few times, trying to keep a real cry from escaping, he trembled. There was a weight removed. Like a curtain being ripped open. It was refreshing and exhilarating but left him feeling naked.

"I haven't ever wanted to acknowledge this before. I hate to admit this," he said looking up and catching a glimpse of Scott's thoughtful expression, feeling soothed, "But when I heard you came out, I felt jealous? I was mad that I didn't have the courage. That you beat me to it? Not that it's a competition, obviously!" he laughed a bit, hands shaking.

"But I just felt like, *Jesus Jay, why can't you handle that?* Like I know my folks would be okay with it, you know? Maybe a bit shocked.... but, now I think about it, maybe not shocked. I've just, I don't know, I've lived here my whole life and the idea of coming out makes me feel like I've been lying to everyone".

The words fell from Jay's mouth quickly. Fear caving away as fast as the tears slid down his cheeks.

"You're not lying. You're just finding your truth, as silly as it sounds. And, I would never pressure anyone to come out or anything, but what I've learned is that being scared is one of the most freeing things I've ever felt," Scott smiled thoughtfully, scooping ice cream into his mouth.

Jay sat in silence, soaking in the words as Scott described his situation. He told Jay about his discussion with his mom and siblings. How he felt so *wrong*, he was getting depressed and was unable to focus on his drumming or school. And when he finally let go of what everyone thought, it was able to feel the most like himself as he ever had. His story was long, really smart and inspiring. Jay listened intently, realizing that everyone had their own struggle. And sometimes you're your own biggest critic.

They had their coffees filled, the night got darker.

Soon their conversation drifted away from being gay to video games, sports, music, and movies. They drifted down a lane of friends, and it was easy. They had just developed an easy friendship, built fully on honesty. It was refreshing.

The waitress appeared again, bringing them their check, "Sorry to break up the party fellas, but I have to kick you out soon. We close in 10," she held up two thumbs up in confirmation and flashed a small smirk.

Scott pulled out his wallet, "I got this! Now that I have captured you for...." he checks his phone, "3 hours! Holy cow. We talked for a long time!"

"Are you sure? I can pay you back!"

"Nope, nope. You get the snacks next time."

"Next time?" Jay smiled flirtatiously, feeling giddy.

*Oh my god. Who am I? Openly flirting with boys in public.*

"I was hoping I'd run in to you at Homecoming maybe. We could, like, awkwardly stand by the punch bowl together and maybe judge people's dancing?" Scott grinned and leaned back after dropping a twenty-dollar bill on to the table.

"That...would be nice. Can we, uh, can we exchange numbers? I think it's going to be my time to step into the ring of outed gayness soon and I would really enjoy knowing I have someone to talk to.... if that's not weird" Jay mumbled.

*How was one supposed to ask for someone's number without sounding desperate? Is that possible?*

"Oh, of course. It would be weird if you didn't ask. I did buy you ice cream, for God's sakes and kidnapped you and asked you to hang out again. It's only right to exchange numbers".

They swapped phones and entered their information slid out of the plastic brown booth.

Still joking and laughing, they made their way through the wind and sleet. A tipsy girl in ripped jeans stumbled past them towards the bar a few doors down, a cop drove quickly through town on the way to the nearby police station, the lights flashing menacingly.

Jay and Scott touched shoulders, intentionally this time, as they light-headedly swayed to the car. Jay was drunk with relief and motivation and an overdose of caffeine with Scott supporting and steadying his shaky hand.

# PART SEVEN

*Lyss*

# CHAPTER 23

A small ribbon of light waves its way into a large, white bedroom. Sheer curtains sway lightly as the heating ducts flick on, making the soft fabric dance majestically, forcing the light to play on the walls and drip into Lyss Roger's eyes as she softly stirs in her massive bed.

Lyss is jammed between approximately 300 cushy pillows that cover almost every inch of the sleep space. And even though she wiggles around in her castle of dreams, the alarm on her iHome starts to talk to her, signaling time to wake up.

She grunts and tugs a pillow hard onto the top of her head, as the early morning DJ begins his happy upbeat announcements for the morning.

"Goooooooodddddddmorning PARTY PEOPLE! It's Friday morning, but don't let your heart weep with the rain that's sure to come down today, we'll be keeping you up and warm alllll day and night long. DJ Spark is spinning TONIGHT at Club Mess. Here's a *taste of what's to come tonight. Keep your heads high friends, because tonight is gonna be a BLAST"*

A sped up, club version of a Taylor Swift song starts to play, with far too much bass and screeching. It's enough to wake anyone up, even Lyss.

Moaning and rolling over in bed, Lyss dangles her tanned legs over the edge of the bed. A loose bun is perched on the side of her head, small pieces tufting out and falling loosely out of place, indicative of restless sleep. She stretches her arms high, left, right and yawns delicately before pursing her lips and slipping off the massive bed and onto the fluffy faux calf skin rug.

Directing her gaze out the window briefly, noting the shitty rain for the day and immediately decides her hair will stay in a bun for the day.

*Not worth it if it's just going to get all fuckin' jacked up.*

Padding lightly to the bathroom, uncurling her chilled toes as she places her feet on the heated floors, and turns the shower on to warm up while analyzing her closet, putting her finger to her lips and other hand on her hip.

The closet, an attachment to the bathroom, has a small chaise lounge in the middle and three walls covered in clothing items. The wall to the left, strictly shoes. Shoes of all types; pumps, wedges, Nike's, boots, Birks. Anything you can possibly imagine is set daintily on the edges of the shelves, facing out, on display for the lovely owner to peruse at her leisure.

The wall facing the entrance to the closet and the right wall, is full of items sorted by article type, they were also color coded. The jackets all hung together from red trench coats and ending with the blackest of leather studded coats. The t-shirts, jeans and blouses all followed the same rule of organization. In the corner sat a hefty four-piece laundry hamper, for expert sorting of color and fabrics for different types of washing cycles. Not that Lyss ever did her own laundry, but she did know how to sort garments.

Lyss touched her pointer finger to her lips while she stood in the middle of the room turning slowly, thinking hard about the day's ensemble. Since she was going to be staying after school and then moving around for her audition, she wanted something cute and comfortable. Especially because she'd get flashier on Saturday night for the big party at Moe's house. Moe always held the largest parties, a certified stoner with access to more booze than necessary.

Moving towards the pants section, she snagged a pair of slim black, high-waist jeans, a cropped Tommy Hilfiger navy blue pull over, and her black slouchy leather jacket. On the way out, she nabs her favorite pair of mid-calf Frye moto boots.

She sets them neatly on the small couch, and strips down and takes a quick shower. She's careful not to get her hair wet while she rinses off and scrubs her face with a Clarisonic.

She steps out of the shower with a wave of steam issuing behind her. Slipping on a silk robe, she plops down at the vanity and starts to work on her face.

Bouncing beauty sponges, swipes of pigments and sweeps of slick liner done masterfully, after which she pulls her hair into a sleek top knot. Her hair is just now long enough to pull it all the way up into a bun. It had been her go to hair style for the last week or so.

Last year, she had chopped off about 11 inches into a cute and edgy bob cut. Everyone had been shocked and so impressed with her new look. It felt very hip and chic at the time, but then like three girls on the Bachelor got the same cut as Lyss and Khloe Kardashian. So now Lyss was a bit over it and was thrilled that it was long enough to style again. (Not without the help of many hair oils and morning vitamins.)

She dressed quickly and checked her phone for the time. She clasped on her lucky necklace, a thin bronze chain with a small stone dangling from the end around her neck and snagged her shoulder bag filled with school supplies and her Mac Book Air, which she insisted on using in class for notes.

She toed her way down the elegant staircase, skimming through her text messages as she went; most of which were from her pompous, idiot friends, who she put up with because they worshipped her, and that felt good. In that entitled and disappointing way. Is it really that great to have people be obsessed with you if they are completely personality-less morons?

There was a random message from Derek Wilms, a douchey jock character that was, well, perfect for her in a traditional 80's movie sense, but she wasn't interested. And seeing him look stupid when he vied for her attention was almost comical.

The thing about Lyss, was she was entitled, yes. She was beautiful, wealthy and had endless opportunities, yes. But she was smart. She understood people, even though she pretended not to. She knew she played up the rich bitch act, but she was allowed to, she didn't have to be real with anyone and she liked it like that. If she had it her way, she'd sit by herself at lunch, take photography classes and avoid the issue of social status, but her entire family didn't work like that. This was how she'd grown up.

"Be the best. Stomp on everyone else. Don't let your guard down" her mother had said, rattling off her 3 rules of life. This was practically engrained in Lyss's DNA.

As she stepped down the stairs and into the ornate, white marbled kitchen, her mother shrieked loudly into her massive iPhone.

"Are you fucking KIDDING ME, BILL? NO. That's not going to work. I need more time with the client and I refuse TO LOSE THIS CASE" she tossed half a cup of coffee down her throat, not even acknowledging Lyss, who rolls her eyes, grabbing a banana. Her mother glanced down at her phone to see another incoming call and switched the line without telling this so-called, 'Bill'.

"Karen, hi! Mind if I put you on hold really quick. I've got a dick on the other line" and before waiting for her answer she flicked back to Bill's line.

After a few more moments her mother finally noticed Lyss as she is throwing away her peel and picks up a pad of paper and scribbles a note to Lyss.

*How's my princess?*

And smiles while she points at the paper for Lyss to look. Lyss read, nods and gives a halfhearted smile.

Her mother barely pays attention to the response before writing again.

*Auditions today? Don't disappoint me.*

And taps the pad multiple times for emphasis a tight smile plastered to her overly botoxed mug. As Lyss tightens her lips and Mrs. Roger's goes back to screaming into her phone about how dumb Bill is.

Lyss sweeps up her bag and storms out to her luxury car in the garage. She opens the door and sighs loudly.

*What a bitch. She finds ways to pay attention to everything but the family. Like, I could do so much more than just acting or singing. I don't even like it anymore.*

As she pulls out and starts to drive, she turns on some pop music with catchy lyrics and thinks out loud to herself. Self-pep talks were necessary when living with a high strung, high end divorce attorney and a father whose business is as mysterious as he is.

"Okay, Lyss. Don't let her ruin your day. You're hot, talented, blonde and bitchin'" She repeated this to herself.

*At least my stupid "friends" will back up that notion when I get to school.*

She got a prime parking spot near the entrance to the school, sticks the car into park, and swiftly strides into the school, trying her best to avoid puddles and rain droplets, not that it would matter. The Frye boots were waterproof.

When she enters, she wipes at the sleeves of her jacket,

as a group of nicely dressed gals appear, as if out of nowhere, to greet her.

They immediately compliment her outfit, and her heart swells for a moment before dropping.

*It's not like the clothes actually matter, they just say what they think I want to hear.*

The girls usher her into the hallway where their lockers reside and douse her in gossip. Something about the drummer from band coming out. Then the conversation shifts to the audition for the play that afternoon.

Lyss listens intently, as the girls divulge information about who is supposedly trying out for the different parts in the show and someone finally says, "I think that one goofy girl, what's her name, with the long blonde hair and the bike? I think I heard Mr. Ashburn encouraging her to try out for one of the leads part the other day in our drama class. Her name was on the list this morning when I went to double check".

Lyss spun around quickly to look at the girl.

"Who? You mean Tristan? No way," she cackled, "She can't possible keep her head on straight long enough to hold a tune" and with that, she flounced away. Leaving the gaggling group of girls to look after her longingly and wade in her cool-ness.

In reality Lyss knew that Tristan had a pretty damn good voice and her charisma was evident and contagious. Which could benefit her in this case, despite how much of an oddball she was. It helped that she was best friends with Sierra Simons, ASB President and fashion guru model type. Not that her social standing had anything to do with Mr. Ashburn's decision, but if he had been encouraging her to tryout, then he must know she had a knack for music. Nervousness crept through her.

*If I don't get this part, how would I explain that to mom? Wait, stop. You'll get it. Positivity and a badass attitude, remember. Always.*

Lyss pushed the thoughts out of her mind. Feeling preemptively competitive. Maybe it would be a good thing if she didn't get the lead, then she might have some time to focus on new hobbies, but her mother would never go for that.

She shook the thoughts away as she lowered herself into the school seats in her first class of the day and chatted animatedly with her neighbors.

# CHAPTER 24

M id school day was coming quick and Lyss checked her phone before the bell rang, where she rolled her eyes once again and she noticed a message from the caveman himself. Derek. Purposefully not reading it, she swiped it away. If he saw she read it, he'd just text again.

Strolling toward the lunch room, she plopped down with her girlfriends and nibbled on her prepped salad and apple chips and listened to the girls rattle on and on about their boring, mundane high school lives.

Lyss managed to keep the scowl off her face, while she leaned her head on her hand. She was just starting to zone out when a hand grabbed her shoulder and she quickly righted herself and turned around to see Derek's meaty face looking down at her. A smile stamped on, his hair slicked back and his letterman's jacket looking just as clean as ever.

*Ugh, eye roll.*

"Aye bae!" he grins at her and winks or, rather,

attempts to. It only comes off as a disappointing twitch, quite irksome.

Lyss stands up and starts tugging at the sleeve of her leather jacket. *If I stand up, at least I won't feel so small and powerless next to him*, she thought. *It's time to put this to rest. No more nice, sweet Lyss.*

"Hi, Derek. How are you?" she smiles lightly, while glancing around the lunch room.

She catches the eye of Simon. The cute alternative boy in her grade. Simon is always swimming in hoodies, cracking jokes, getting into fights with the rich kids and riding his bike around town.

Lyss had noticed that he frequently made a point to chat with her and make eye contact when he could. While she wouldn't admit it aloud, she liked it. His flirting tactics were unusual for high school boys she knew and the intensity in his eyes made her stomach jump. He was endearing in Lyss's opinion. Even though he got into a lot of arguments with people, she could appreciate someone who fought for equal treatment and didn't take shit. Take shit the way she did.

Her face heated up and she cursed her light complexion for giving away her embarrassment, when seeing Simon. Tearing her eyes away, she forced herself to look at Derek again, who has somehow launched into a story about homecoming the following weekend.

*Oh, what a fairytale he lives in. How does he not notice that I'm a million miles away?*

"So, what color corsage should I get you? I don't know if you've even told me what color dress you're wearing" he ends with, looking proud. He probably had to google the word corsage before lunch, so he didn't look like a fool. Though that was inevitable.

"Uhm–I'm sorry. What? What did you say?" she shakes her head, scrunching up her face as she decides whether or not she hears him properly.

"Homecoming, pretty little thang. We're going together, yeah? Soo what color are you wearing?" he wiggles his eyebrows at her and touches her shoulder again. A cringe and shutter springs through her.

She dips her arm down, so that his hand falls off her.

"No," she says slowly, anger overcoming her confusion.

"What?" he snaps, a flash of anger disrupting his otherwise hilariously jock, meat head, face.

"I said, 'no'. I'm not going to homecoming with you. So, it's no business of yours what I'll be wearing to the dance, if I even decide to go".

The girls at her table gasp at the last part. God forbid

Lyss not go to the dance. Then snicker quietly, which just feeds Lyss's bitchy side and annoys her further.

*Why am I so all over the place with my emotions? I like the attention, I don't. Back and forth. Ugh.*

"I thought we were a thing?" Derek snaps back, blinking wildly.

"No, we aren't. I'm sorry if you ever got that impression. But I'm not interested. But I'm sure someone would be happy to go with you. You still have a *whole* week to find the lucky girl" she replies, lifting her eyebrows, sarcasm dripping from her voice and expression.

He looks at her, shocked and shaking his head slightly.

"Good luck, and" she says in mock joyousness and pumping her fist "have a good weekend", spinning around to take a seat again.

She glances at Simon, again. Who half nods at her, still looking at her as the commotion grew momentarily and she tucks her head down, as chills run down her spine.

Derek stalks away, no doubt going to tell his buddies they would hook up. He'd be a jerk about the whole thing. But Lyss felt good, despite potential Twitter drama. Being a bitch can be helpful. The girls erupt into giggles and a few slow claps. She flashes a smile and adjusts her necklace, out of habit.

*I wish I could be a total asshole to the people that matter.*

# CHAPTER 25

The last bell of the day buzzes bleakly. Students smile and mill about aimlessly as they chatter with friends, make plans for the weekend and begin to unwind and forget all the days' lessons.

Lyss scoops up her notebooks and laptop, with her beautiful scrawl all over the pages and lightly places them in her bag and headed toward the stairs to the lower level of the school.

Her friends greet her in the common area of the school, as always. They giggled and talked, like all the others, about plans for the weekend. Lyss listened absently, her sarcastic smile splayed half-heartedly on her face. She was only partially listening to the girls, too focused on thinking about the auditions.

"Lyss, you ready to head to the drama room? I can't WAIT to see your performance. It's gonna be so flippin' good" one of her blonde, big headed friends said as she sidled up next to Lyss and hooked their arms together.

"Oh, yeah. It'll be a blast. Can't wait to blow some minds" she mumbled snidely, pulling lightly at her stone necklace.

"Totally. Did we ever find out if that silly little blonde chick was auditioning?" the girl said as she whipped her phone out of her back pocket and studied a text that had just come through.

"Um- no. No. I have no idea. We'll see. But I'm not too worried about it" Lyss responded with a confidence that reminded her of really good fake leather. Only she knew the difference between its authenticity and faux-ness.

They strode along the hallways together, arms still linked and Lyss began to sweat when they neared the arts wing.

She couldn't help but think about the lead part, the need to win was instilled in her. Her parents were competitive people, and even though the play didn't matter to her, she still had an edge in her approach. Disappointing her family wasn't an option. But it wasn't what she wanted. The play didn't matter to her at all, actually.

There were some programs she had been googling that happened at the local community college in the evenings for some film photography classes, she thought about approaching her mother about them but hadn't worked up the confidence she needed. So, instead, here she was. Back in the drama department.

Lyss pushed these thoughts out of her mind, as they got closer to the drama department.

*Just keep it together. This is what I've worked for, what my mother has paid for me to work on. This is the dream, the goal. You'll have time for hobbies later. Right now, you must get into the acting programs in New York.*

They pushed the doors open, and Lyss and her friend joined a few other drama regulars in the corner. Propping herself up and crossing her arms to glare at people as they walk in to the room, this was her key intimidation stance. To portray confidence, is to be confident. Her mother instilled this attitude in her when she was a kid, too. She wasn't supposed to cry, to show any soft spots. Another rule her mother abided by, she claimed it's what made her so successful.

Mr. Ashburn came tumbling through the doors and clapped his hands together. He started to drone on in his usual hokey voice, trying to encourage and remain positive, blah blah blah.

Lyss always thought he seemed small and weak. Having worked with him the previous season, she could sense his entire resolve shake when she confronted him about issues. He was a newer teacher and Lyss used that to her advantage. She didn't bully him, per se, but she certainly didn't let herself get bullied, either. Assertiveness, another admired trait in the Rogers' household.

Mr. Ashburn continued to talk and Lyss continued to tune him out, fully disrespecting his speech. She'd heard it all before. They'd break up into teams, do auditions, he'd hopefully announce the parts tonight. And then they could go home. It was always the same damn thing. Every. Single. Time.

One of the girls whispered next to her and giggled. Everyone knew that the girls in their grade were particularly obsessed with Mr. A. And it seemed that the quirky blonde girl, Tristan was zoned out in a completely different way. Gazing at Mr. A as if she was going to start drooling. Lyss chuckled along with the girls beside her, who were poking fun at the little hearts forming in Tristan's eyes, as Mr. A tried to avoid looking at her, obviously feeling uncomfortable with the unwarranted attention he was receiving.

Pretty soon, the crowd broke up into their audition groups. The regular drama kids went and picked out prime spots in the audience, so they could watch and analyze (A. K. A. make fun of) the other students who were going out for the different parts.

Typically, the people who wanted to have smaller roles went first, as there were more of them, and the casting could be done quickly, as Mr. Ashburn could usually give them the random roles they selected. Then they'd move on to the larger parts after taking a quick break.

Lyss and her friends yawned their way through some tremendously boring auditions. Some students simply falling in to small talking roles, while others took some medium sized singing and acting roles.

Most people were regulars to the drama department, but none of them had the training that Lyss had.

When she was young she had begged her parents to let her join some ballet classes, do voice training and begin to act in small local productions. Her mother quickly caught on to the raw talent and soul that Lyss had, and threw her swiftly into every club, and private lesson she could get Lyss in to. A great way to monopolize on a talent. Which ended up ruining the entire process of acting and singing for her. All the seriousness had stolen the fun and excitement from the entire thing. But here Lyss sat, arms crossed, judging others, becoming competitive but wishing she was anywhere but here.

The family spent copious amounts of their money, not

that the money mattered, on her training, and the Roger's family now boastfully gushed about their daughter who was "such a star". They expected her to use the training, to get into a good school for acting and singing and end up on Broadway. It was the only version of life they could imagine for their daughter that involved the arts. Nothing else would be good enough for their "talented little girl".

This instilled fear of failing, of not being the best, sometimes brought out the worst in Lyss. Deep down, no, she wasn't a raging bitch. But to keep herself on top and out of her mother's way, she had to be. Being the vain, pushy girl, she acted as, wasn't who she was. She didn't want an uproar. Another slap to the face in the name of defeat. She simply needed to maintain her skills, get the parts and she wouldn't have to fight her way out of the house. Despite her interests in other activities and hobbies, she had to stay focused on what were, as she had been told, the most important things.

So, when the break rolled around, and she had to start preparing for her solo audition, she glanced around nervously for Tristan.

Tristan was a total spaz, but even Lyss had to admit, Tristan seemed so simple in the best way. Approachable, easy going and free. In addition to her obsession for Mr. Ashburn and her willingness to do whatever she had to do to be close to him, Lyss saw Tristan as a valid threat for the latest auditions.

When the group reconvened, they were ready to start the casting process for the few main characters, most of the crew and other new cast members sat around in the chairs to watch the fun tryouts for the leads. Some boys splayed out over a few auditoriums seats or propped their legs up on the chairs in front of them. While the girls sat crisscross on the floor. One set of freshmen girls were braiding each other's hair as they eagerly awaited the next few songs.

The boys went first and Lyss tugged gently on her necklace, nerves tickling her stomach as she pulled out her script and music sheets again to recall the lines from the song they were required to sing.

It was finally her turn, and Mr. Ashburn turned around from his seat.

"Ready, Lyss? It's all yours!" with a pleasant but annoying smile.

She pushed her shoulders back without smiling back, as feigning confidence helped to exude the feeling, and she strutted up the stairs to do her part. When the music began, she looked right at the back of the room, avoiding any eye contact she could. The eye contact wasn't a problem when the real production happened, mainly because you're blinded by the lights for most of it, but auditions were dim, and she could make out everyone's faces, which made her more insecure.

Lyss knew the words, she knew the inflections and the correct hand motions to make, so she did it. She sang loud, and high and felt supremely good about her performance. She did all the right things, but she couldn't help but wonder if anyone could tell that her heart wasn't in it. She felt robotic, just doing what she was supposed to. But they erupted with applause as soon as she finished, so apparently most of her classmates didn't have a good bullshit detector. Or they simply wanted her approval.

Slapping a grin on her face and walking off stage, she looked around quickly to find Tristan, pouring over her papers, trying to remember the words to the song. She seemed completely unfazed by Lyss's grandiose performance.

"Alright, next up is...." Mr. A trailed off, consulting his list, "Tristan. You ready?"

Tristan snapped her head up right and shoved her papers in between the auditorium seats, wiped her palms rapidly on her light wash jeans, tripping her way on to the stage, mumbling as she went.

Lyss crossed her arms and tipped her hip sideways, glowering at her from down below. She knew, full well, that

Tristan could see the crowd, so she wanted to make it clear that she was judging her hard.

But Tristan didn't make eye contact, not with anyone, instead, she closed her eyes gently, and sang.

She belted out the tune, with passion and force. And if Lyss was more outwardly emotional, her jaw would have dropped.

As Tristan's version of the song wrapped up, the entirety of the crew and cast just gawked at Tristan, one side of her mouth curled up into a half smiled as she shrugged and stumbled back off stage.

Mr. Ashburn was clearly shocked at the sheer talent, and just managed a, "Wow, Tristan. Thanks that was lovely".

She had plopped back down; a few girls had patted her on the back and she just sunk into her regular old self. Lyss watched her, furious. It seemed her shot at getting the lead, may have just slipped out of her hands.

Before leaving for the evening, Mr. Ashburn promised to give them the results and parts before the weekend. So, the students milled about, waiting for Mr. A and the rest of the teachers' results. As Lyss was checking her phone for messages and the time, she saw Mr. Ashburn appear quietly and before he went to put up the cast list, he strode over to Lyss.

Lyss saw his approach and her stomach sank, he'd

never come over to congratulate her before. Why would he start now?

"Hey, Lyss. So, before I put this up, I wanted to have a quick conversation with you about the parts. There are a few parts in this production that are large, but not necessarily the lead but I think it might behoove you to try some other things..." he started, but she cut him off.

"Spit it out. What are you saying?" she was quaking with anger and talking through gritted teeth. She just wanted to hear the words.

"Uhm- we're, uh, going to be giving Tristan the lead" he said, eyeing her nervously.

She flipped.

"ARE YOU FUCKING KIDDING ME?" Lyss demanded, voice at full volume.

Students around them turned around to stare and take in the new and very real scene.

"GOOD LUCK PUTTING ON A GOOD SHOW WITH YOUR COMMUNITY COLLEGE DEGREE AND SUB-PAR LEAD" she screamed, throwing her arms in the direction of Tristan and her rag tag group of hipster friends. Her brows knit close together, her face hot and her legs shaking.

Lyss knew she was overreacting, but no one knew what she did to deserve this, no one knew what her family expected of her and someone had to take the blame. The pressure she felt daily had her finally blowing up, turning in to a harpy, and deranged anger machine. And she needed to excuse herself before she made a complete fool of herself and her reputation.

"Excuse me," she mumbled suddenly.

Spinning around quickly, she snatched up her bag, held on to her necklace and strode calmly out of the drama room, careful not to let any anger build up in the form of tears.

As soon as she was out of the room and few feet away, she let the hot tears spring to her ducts, she pushed her hand to her eyes as she stomped swiftly toward the only private bathroom in school.

The hallways were empty. Her boots slapped the tiled floor with tremendous footfalls that reverberated down the hall. She briefly heard a door shut and assumed it was a teacher leaving late.

Approaching the private bathroom, she flung the door open and quickly slammed it behind her, pushing it closed and fastening the lock. The light was already on in the bathroom, which was odd. There was a little animated sign inside by the light switch that read, "save energy, turn off the light!" and everyone usually did. She thought about it only briefly, before sinking to the floor. Letting her jeans hit the dirty floor and her bag slip off her shoulder.

Tucking her knees in to her chest, she wrapped her arms around her legs, hugging herself into a tight ball and cried. She heaved and moaned and swore. She wept for a solid ten minutes before letting her sobs slowly peter out. She closed her eyes and thought to herself.

*Why are you even crying like this? Who cares if mom is even disappointed in you? You're always disappointed in her. It's time to admit to her what you want.... maybe this is a blessing in disguise. Maybe not. You'll be grounded. You'll get dirty looks and snide comments about how fat you are now, which is probably why you didn't get the role. Whatever, she's a fucking bitch.*

Lyss just swam in her thoughts for a few moments, controlling her breathing. She blew her nose and finally hoisted herself to stand. She stared in the mirror and dabbed at her mascara absent mindedly. The bathroom was generally cleaner in here than the regular women's bathroom. And most girls liked to use it when they had an emergency or needed to change, but today it smelled of vomit and vanilla perfume. Lyss was starting to get a headache.

She glanced at her phone as she picked up her bag. A few messages from her friends popped up and her mother send a message, as well.

Idiot 1: Holy shit. Nice one gurl. You totes deserve the part.

Idiot 2: OMG where are you?

Mom: Working late. I expect good news in the morning.

She closed her eyes once more, did a double take at her makeup, lightly touched her hair, making sure it was still in place and strode out of the bathroom. Bee-lining for the parking lot so she could finally go home to be alone.

# CHAPTER 26

Flinging the exit door open and dredging numbly towards her car, Lyss shoved her phone into the back pocket of her jeans. She ignored all messages and simply wanted some time to herself. The best thing about her group of friends was that they'd actually leave her alone if she didn't respond.

Because they didn't really care if she was okay, they just wanted to make sure they didn't miss any gossip.

She slipped into her car, bag in passenger seat and rested her forehead to the steering wheel, taking a few deep breaths and feeling grateful that she wouldn't see her mother that evening. And now, it was time to relax. To move on and try to forget about Tristan.

Flicking through Spotify, she chose an indie music playlist and adjusted the volume to a reasonable level. Then weaved out of the school lot, ready for the weekend and needing a bubble bath more than ever.

The trees swayed more fiercely than they had this

morning, the wind picked up and the rain began to pelt her windshield more heavily. She flicked the handle on the right side of her steering wheel to accelerate the wipers, her windshield blurring steadily.

Humming carefully and zoning out slightly, she drove the familiar road on the side of the school and towards home. The drive was always relaxing when it was empty.

Lots of trees and the mellow glowing street lights. The rain felt cozy and fitting for Lyss's confusing mood and emotions.

The rain pounded harder on the windshield, causing Lyss to squint at the road as the headlights illuminated the space in front of the car.

Trees shook, leaves fell and . . .figures lined the road?

*Wait what am I seeing?* Lyss thought, pushing her head closer to the front, crunching her nose as she tried to make out the shapes she was seeing on the side of the road.

*What the hell is this? Those are people. What could they possibly be doing outside in this weather?*

She flicked the lock button for the door handles and slowed down, like everyone who sees a car crash, trying to make out the details, while simultaneously not caring. The waving figure had moved towards the road, arms flying with urgency.

*Oh great, a crazy person. I don't need to get kidnapped right now.*

She slowed down more and recognized the square backpack and kinky blonde hair bouncing manically behind. It was Tristan.

*Goddamit. What'd she pop a bike tire?*

Lyss came to a stop, there were no street lights nearby. So, Tristan was drowning in wet, cold and darkness.

"Um- what are y-" Lyss started.

"Hey, hey! Oh my god. Thanks so much for stopping. Holy Shit. Oh my god. It's Sierra. Sierra, she's fainted. I-can you help? I need a hospital" Tristan spat, looking frazzled, and wide eyed, and then Lyss noticed a lump of a person, covered in mud, slumped over on the ground.

"Shit!" Lyss shouted, unclicking her seatbelt immediately and unlocking the door and jumping out of the car.

The two girls heaved Sierra up from under her limp arms, she was breathing, lightly and strained. Sierra was covered in mud, shivering from the wind whipping at her soaked frame. The two girls dragged her to the car. They slid her into the back seat as gently as possible but with as much haste as they could manage. And Tristan launched herself into the backseat with her best friend. Laying Sierra's head onto her lap. Dirt coated the backseat.

"To the hospital please??" she shouted, her brows touching in the middle and tears sliding down her flushed cheeks. Lyss had never seen, nor before then, could she imagine Tristan in a state such as this. Completely flustered and scared. Lyss took off, pulling a U-turn.

Tristan slid her backpack off quickly and rummaged around, finding the handle of a small water bottle. She propped Sierra's head up again, who was slowly becoming conscious. Groaning slightly with every lurch the car made.

"Sierra. Hey, hey, Sierra. Drink this. You passed out. I'm taking you to the hospital. I'll call your mom as soon as we get there," Tristan said in a slower voice than before, the calmness rushing back. Staying strong and controlling the meek quaver in her voice.

There was some mumbling and Tristan tipped the bottle back for Sierra to sip lightly.

The entire back seat of the car was now covered in water and mud and blood, which seemed to be trickling out of Tristan's palm. Foot prints stamped along the seat and smeared along the floor, and Lyss drove as fast as she could to the hospital. Which, luckily was close by and right next door to the police station, too.

"Thank you so much" Tristan said, glancing up from

Sierra and toward the rearview mirror, where Lyss's eyes darted back at her.

"No problem, glad I was driving by".

"I've been so worried about her. She stresses. Avoids eating. I thought she was being smarter with her body...." she mentioned quickly before she trailed off. Now wasn't the time for an explanation.

"She'll be okay. She'll get help" Lyss said reassuringly, panting with stress as they screeched to a halt outside of the hospital. A man on duty was standing outside to assist people who needed help upon arrival.

Lyss jumped out and motioned for him to help, although he was already making his way to the car.

"She passed out on the road, she needs help".

Tristan nodded confirmation and the man rushed over to help extract the limp but stirring Sierra out of the back seat.

He put her in the nearest wheel chair and slipped Sierra down the hall and said to the girls, "go to the front. Any info you have will be helpful" gesturing to the desk nearby and disappeared with Sierra.

# CHAPTER 27

The two girls finally started toward the car. But only after a long talk detailing the evenings events with the necessary people and Tristan drooling over a male nurse who picked the remaining glass out of her hand before bandaging her.

Tristan had rushed to talk with the nurses. Giving them all of Sierra's personal information and her folks' phone numbers. Tristan texted Sierra's mom with one hand while explaining the situation out loud. Sierra's mom magically turned up within what felt like a few minutes and gave them both long hard hugs. Tristan had a tearful conversation with their family in the corner and Lyss suspected they talked about Sierra's unhealthy habits.

Tristan batted her eyelashes at a male nurse who gave them an update on Sierra's vitals and thanked them for being so helpful and quick. She was going to be okay.

The girls hardly had a chance to talk to each other the

whole time and now, leaving the hospital, they were finally alone.

"So, uhm, thanks for the help. I know that wasn't like, the most radical or ideal Friday night" Tristan said, glancing at Lyss cautiously, giving her a meek smile.

"No, it's fine. Glad I could help. Pretty sure your bike handle bars wouldn't have done the trick" she said, half smiling and bumping into Tristan playfully, as they trudged through the parking lot. Lightening the mood seemed necessary, it had been a tense evening. The rain began to let up.

Lyss had gone to park the car once Tristan had run inside after the nurse wheeled Sierra inside. She had parked in a spot towards the back of the visitors' lot, bordering on the edge of the police departments designated spots.

Tristan gave her an odd look, of confusion and a slight smile. She was obviously confused by Lyss's friendlier nature.

"I hope she'll be okay. I said it earlier, but I've been so worried about Sierra. She takes life so seriously, you know? Always planning, she's her own biggest critic. Eating has taken a back seat, you know?" Tristan said, kicking a rock, "Could you also maybe not mention this to anyone? I don't think Sierra would be super happy to have everyone know about this..."

"Oh god. Of course not," she mimed zipping her lips.

"Thanks. I appreciate it. I'm not used to going into full stress mode, man. I don't think I've ever been compelled to move that fast in my whole life, I'm like still shaking," she chuckled, holding up her arm.

"Dude! I don't think I've ever seen you looking so frantic and I've been in school with you since elementary, but you handled it so well. And Sierra's a smart girl, she'll be alright. She's in good hands. It's cool, though, that you're so laid back about life. I wish I was more like that" Lyss said, feeling comfortable. Tristan was easy to be around. The sensitive subject dropped momentarily and Tristan switched gears.

"So, are you mad at me? The play...and all. I mean, I didn't mean to take your part, you know" Tristan suddenly spat back at Lyss, she seemed nervous and awkward about it.

"I know. I know," Lyss waved her hand and rolled her eyes at Tristan, "No worries. I just have a weird family who like expects the best of me, blah blah blah. It might actually be, like, a blessing in disguise. I need to finally own up to my passion not being acting, finally".

Tristan nodded in understanding and waited for Lyss to continue.

"I just, they think I should be this *star* or something

ridiculous like that. I don't really like it anymore, though. Acting and singing was a passion I had as a kid. Am I really supposed to take advantage of that my whole life?" she said, letting the words spill, "That's rhetorical. I know the answer. I just feel like I'm always being this bitchy person that I don't feel like I truly am".

"I feel that. I'm surprised, I guess. You seem a lot more chill outside of school. Like, easy to talk to, funny and not nearly as intimidating as I always thought....in a good way!" Tristan said.

"Intimidating?" Lyss laughed, "Thanks. I guess I'm just not really myself at school. Or, anywhere for that matter. And you seem easy to be around. And Sierra too. No wonder you two are so close. And again, I'm so sorry about what happened. I know she'll be okay, but that was like, the most terrifying moment" Lyss shook her head.

"I know. She stresses. She takes on too much, I try to calm her down, make her see that life is more than planners and events. But, she doesn't care. You know? *She* controls her life and there's no arguing with it. She goes too far. Her eating has become so scarce. She's strong, too which makes it hard to talk about. And she's supportive. She needs to realize that she needs help now" Tristan nodded to herself, staring at the ground.

"Yeah...I suppose it's hard to admit when you need help. Like, easier said than done, right? But taking care of yourself is important." Lyss said as they neared the guest parking space that Lyss had found earlier.

As they stepped up to the car, red and blue lights came flying up to the station. Tristan paused, squinting at the police car.

"What's up?" Lyss asked, noticing Tristan's distraction.

"I think that's my pops" she half smiled, "Mind if I say hey?"

Lyss gave Tristan a thumb up and pocketed her keys as they walked a few more aisles to the station. What was another few minutes in the cold rain at this point?

"Hope it's nothing serious" Tristan said as they got close to the car.

Her dad stepped out, a big guy and saw his daughter.

"T! What are you doing here?" he said jovially but rustling his hair in confusion, realizing their location.

She nudged her thumb at the hospital and gave him a grave look with wide eyes.

"Can we talk about it tonight? Friend stuff. Sierra had a bit of a meltdown, literally. I'd rather be sitting when we talk about it. I'll be home for din" she said, and he looked slightly concerned. But accepted her response, eyeing her muddy clothes and dripping makeup.

"Sure hon. I got to get this troublemaker kid out. Hold on, one sec" and he strolled to the other side of the car.

And out popped Simon Matthews.

Lyss immediately felt her face grow hot.

"Heya Tristan! And.....oh, hey Lyss" Simon said with a sly smile. "I'm a full-fledged criminal now."

Tristan's dad laughed, "Haven't seen this kid in a while and this is how I catch up with him. I hear he's buddying up with you for homecoming next week! That's great!"

Lyss looked back and forth between Tristan and her dad, completely befuddled. Then slightly jealous when hearing Simon was joining Tristan at the dance.

"Sounds like it! But what the hell did you do? Will you even be able to go to homecoming?" Tristan said, covering her smile with her hand.

"He took off with some dick head kid's fancy car. Deserved it. But I do have to call this one's folks. I'll try to ease the blow the best I can" Tristan's dad supplied with a shrug, "He's just lucky I was in the area when the call came in"

Simon shrugged too and winked at Lyss one last time,

"Well ladies, go get cleaned up and have a good weekend. Let's catch up soon" he said and saluted them as he stalked inside the station with Tristan's dad.

"T, we're talking about this hospital business when I get home" Mr. Pedersen said sternly over his shoulder.

"Of course. See you at home" Tristan said.

The girls swung back around, giving each other exasperated looks.

"So, you know Simon well?" Lyss asked

"Yeah, he's a good bud. He was best friends with my brother growing up, and because we were the same age, we always had things in common, he's like a free additional brother, really. He's wonderfully weird. Our friend groups are going to homecoming together next week, I think. Or, I guess we'll see now. Why, you got a thing for him?"

Lyss hesitated before responding, "Yeah, yeah. I think I do" and smiled at Tristan.

"So, since we're like friends or whatever now, want to join us at homecoming next week and maybe see a movie tonight? I'd happily play cupid for you and Simon and to pay for the popcorn. We could do dinner at my folks', I need to tell them what happened at minimum and could probably use the support" Tristan said, wringing her hands together and grimacing slightly at her own words, "No offense, but I never thought I'd ask you to hang out."

Lyss laughed, "Me neither. But, honestly, I'd love to do a movie and to go to homecoming with you and your friends," she nodded emphatically, "Let's get cleaned up first, go rescue your bike, I think it'll fit in my trunk. We can talk with your parents' then movie it up. I'm, like, oddly excited."

"Cool, me too! I really do appreciate your help and like, the willingness to do all of this," Tristan said, smiling bashfully.

*Wow. This could be a really healthy friendship. Is this actually happening?*

Lyss leaned in to Tristan and pulled her in to a tight hug. Feeling her heart melt three sizes smaller, like the Grinch. Pealing her layers of protection down, slowly.

Tristan pulled away finally, grinning ear to ear.

"Thanks again, Lyss. For helping. I think I can safely say that Sierra will be very appreciative, too".

"Thanks for hanging out tonight. This feels really refreshing despite that extremely stressful and terrifying situation" Lyss finished.

They continued to chat they stalked off to the car. Rain pouring down and mud sliding off their boots.

Kjerstin Lie

# DOWN THE PRIMROSE PATH

Down the Primrose Path Copyright © 2018 by Kjerstin Lie All Rights Reserved.

All rights reserved. No part of this book may be reproduced in any form or by any electronic or mechanical means including information storage and retrieval systems, without permission in writing from the author. The only exception is by a reviewer, who may quote short excerpts in a review.

Cover designed by Marcel Ardans.

This book is a work of fiction. Names, characters, places, and incidents either are products of the author's imagination or are used fictitiously. Any resemblance to actual persons, living or dead, events, or locales is entirely coincidental.

Kjerstin Lie
Visit my website at www.KjerstinLie.com

Printed in the United States of America

First Printing: June 2018

ISBN-13 978-1721167753

Kjerstin Lie

78156817R10159

Made in the USA
Middletown, DE
30 June 2018